A Divine Production
Presents

BOSSES
OF
THE LAND

A Series of Novellas

A Divine Production

ISBN 10: 0985149949
ISBN 13: 978-0-9851499-4-9
Editor: Rubina Sardon
A Divine Production logo by: nicolejaneen@gmail.com
Cover Design by: Dynasty's Visionary Design

Library of Congress Control Number: 2012902636

First Printing February 2012
Printed in the United States of America

10 9 8 7 6 5 4 3 2 1

This novella is a work of fiction. Any references to real people, events, establishments or locals are intended only to give the fiction a sense of reality and authenticity. Other names, characters, and incidents occurring in the work are either the product of the author's imagination or are used fictitiously, as those fictionalized events and incidents that involve real persons. Any character that happens to share the name of a person who is an acquaintance of the author, past or present, is purely coincidental and is in no way intended to be an actual account involving that person.

A Divine Production
Presents

LEGEND

A Novella

By

Shenetta Marie

DEDICATION

This one is for my biggest supporter,
Valarie Roundtree

I truly appreciate everything you do and have done for me.
I know there isn't anyone on the face of this earth that has
my back like you do.
I thank the Lord for blessing me with you, because I
couldn't have asked for a better mom.
Thank you mommy and I love you with all my heart.

ACKNOWLEDGEMENTS

First and foremost I would like to thank God my Lord and Savior. Thank you again for creating Shenetta Marie.

Valarie Roundtree my mommy/sister/best friend

Dwight Quinn III my oldest son also my big monster, Dionté Clemis my youngest son also my lil animal

Tamira Adams-Clemis I LOVE MY SISTER, Sha'Tyah Monae Ballard hey Auntie, James Patrick Sadler Jr. hey nephew, Jaylen Pierre Sadler hey my sister's son

Jimmie Jermale Clemis hey baby brother, Jimmie Jermale Clemis Jr. hey auntie's lil Boo

Jimmie Lee Clemis Jr. hey brother, Janeja Leeshae Clemis hey my brother's daughter

Quantell Thomas-Clemis hey lil bro

Rubina Sardon my best friend/sister, Taylor Shereé Sardon, Tania Shauntille Sardon, Ronae and Ronnelle Drakeford hey God-daughters, Rashad Sincere hey GG's baby

Korrine Quinn hey baby girl, DeAngelo Quinn hey son

Virgil Barshon Hammond Jr. my grandson, V-Team grandma loves you so much, DeMari LaShaé Hudson hey granddaughter, Ashley Carson and Sade Carson hey God-daughters

Enoch Scott III my dear friend, I will love you always.

Tanjenique Travis and Kierra Gayle hey God-daughters

Dwayne Travis my boy, if don't no one else see the good in you, I do.

Iyesha Hill my Cuzo lets hurry up and get your joint out here.

Antonio Coleman thanks for the Spoken Word. You are truly an inspiration; hope to read more of your thoughts.

Once again to everyone who has ever entered and exited my life whether good or bad, because without any of you I wouldn't be who I am today, thanks.

Last but not least thanks to all the Her Promise fans, you all are truly my motivation and I won't keep you waiting too much longer for Sincerely Hers.

Can I

Beautiful,

Can I
Touch you
Feel your feelings
Touch your inner being; being all I can be for you and all you
would want me to be for you

Can I
Be the one who makes you drip from the very thought of me,
of us

Can I
Kiss you in those hidden places that's buried deep within your
heart

Can I
Please touch you if not physically then mentally bringing
forth the thought of the possibility, the chance of me touching
you

Can I?

Spoken Word of,
Antonio Coleman

PROLOGUE

Standing in the corner of a dark parking garage the hunter waited patiently for his prey to arrive. He adjusted the black skully on his head to make sure it was secure. He also made sure the face mask covering his nose and lips was secure. He then pulled the hoodie a little lower over his face so that all could be seen was his piercing dark brown eyes. He gripped his 9mm tightly in his right hand standing very still against the brick wall of the garage waiting for the perfect moment to pounce.

He stalked his intended victim as they pulled their 2011 Ford Taurus SEL in its assigned parking space of the garage then exiting the car.

As his victim walked towards the elevator doors he walked behind them without making any type of sounds. His victim, talked to someone on their cell phone not realizing that they were being followed.

As he got closer he figured he really didn't want to shoot his gun because he had another plan in mind. He tucked his pistol in the waist band of his jeans and pulled out his Benchmade 51 Morpho Bali-Song Butterfly knife. He got as close as he could and grabbed the victims head then slashing their throat. He slid them to the ground and then proceeded to pull out their tongue through the open wound of their throat, giving them a famous Colombian necktie.

The hunter walked away leaving his prey lying on the garage floor dead.

He didn't want to kill; he hated having to get physical. He just wished everybody played by the same set of rules, especially his. If they did then everything would run smoothly. But seeing as though they didn't, this person had to go. Snitching was never an option in the game he was playing and since motherfuckers couldn't control their tongues he gave them a little assistance. But this motherfucker in particular should have known better, they should have known that their life was over the very moment they formed an alliance with the Federal Bureau of Investigations.

And if they didn't know anything at all they should have known that they were fucking with a Boss, and that's exactly what Legend was.

A muthafuckin' Boss of The Land.

ONE

Legend sat outside of the Cocktale Lounge on Superior Avenue waiting for his nigga Quan to pull up, so they could discuss some business. He wasn't planning on going inside the spot because he wasn't the bar type. He didn't like being in enclosed spaces and around a bunch of niggas. And the Cocktale was definitely too small for him with a gang of niggas standing around scheming. Legend actually wasn't a drinker at all anyway. He didn't smoke weed nor did any other type of drug for that matter because he didn't like the feeling of being impaired. He prided his self on being aware of his surroundings at all times. He was a rich nigga and not that hood rich shit niggas be boasting about. So he would be damned if a muthafucka would catch him slipping because he was on some tipsy shit.

When he checked his rearview mirror he noticed his boy Quan stepping out of his car wearing some stupid big ass diamond earrings in his ears and a big dumb ass platinum diamond necklace around his neck. He really did dig the cat Quan, but he didn't care for his flossy ways. He tried explaining to his boy that all that flossy shit only brought attention and not always good attention.

Quan hopped in the passenger seat of Legends car reaching over giving him some dap, "What's good my nigga? I see you over here incognito as always."

"That's the best to be my man. I told you all that flashy shit go' do is make you a target for the jack boys or either the Feds."

"Yeah I hear you talking big man, but I can't be stepping out looking like no bum ass nigga feeling all naked without my jewels. You feel me?"

"I hear what you saying, but trust when I tell you; you can look fly without all that extra shit. But anyway what's up wit' that one thing?"

Quan pulled his visor down so he could check his dreads making sure they were neat and in place, "Everything good. That shit moving like hot cakes. You got everybody eating with those prices. My girl is going to drop that bread off tomorrow. That's cool?"

"Yeah that's what's up," Legend responded reaching out his hand for some dap.

Quan returned the hand gesture then hopped out of the car heading across the street towards the bar so he could go get his sloppy on.

Legend was getting ready to pull off to head home but someone caught his eye. A female wearing some army fatigue low rise skinny cargo pants, a white tank top with the word Sexy in gold letters spread across her voluptuous breast, sporting some wheat wedge Timberland boots. She also rocked a low haircut; he thought that shit was so fucking sexy. He really couldn't get a good look at her face but from what he could see was enough to have him intrigued. She stood on the side walk with a big brown Gucci Hobo bag on her shoulder with her hands in her pockets talking to a nigga he grew up with and did business with. He watched as they exchanged words wondering who she was. Once done with their conversation the female walked away sliding inside of the passenger seat of a black Dodge Charger.

He normally wasn't the inquiring type but he really wanted to know who the female was even though he couldn't get a good look at her face. Her swag alone had him wondering. He got out of the car and walked over to where his boy Horace was standing, freaking a mild.

"What's good Legend? What got you over this way?" Horace asked as he gave Legend some dap.

"Shit really, just got finish fuckin' wit' Quan. But I came over to ask you who that female was you were just talking to?"

Horace smiled at his nigga. As long as he has known Legend he had never seen him with a broad. He chalked it up to him just being such a private person. "That's my nigga Mia. Why?"

"Just curious I guess. I've never seen her around." Legend responded leaning against Horace's car.

"Well that's because she's kind of a private person. I only see her when it's time for us to take care of some business."

Now he was really curious. He wondered what type of business Horace was referring to, "What kind of business you talkin' 'bout?"

Crossing one leg over the other and folding his arms against his chest Horace responded, "I don't know if I should tell you all that. You might try to steal her from me."

Legend gave a slight chuckle, "Man if she some type of prostitute you ain't got to worry about that shit. You know a nigga like me ain't paying a female for shit."

"Nigga I'm just fucking wit yo' ass. She ain't no damn whore. That's my cook. She breaks all my shit down and package everything up for me."

He looked at Horace sideways, "So she in the game?"

"Not really, she just cooks for a couple of dudes, getting her money that way."

Legend nodded his head up and down real slow, "That's what's up."

"What you want me to introduce you to her or something?" Horace asked glad to see his nigga opening up for a change about something.

Walking towards his car Legend replied, "Nah, I'm good my nigga. I'll see her around. We'll cross paths one day.

Legend drove off with the mysterious Mia on his mind. He was really anticipating the day when they really would cross paths. He then pushed Mia to the back of his mind storing her there and focusing on the task at hand, which was getting them bricks ready for distribution.

TWO

Legend got out of his bed bright and early the next morning. After doing a quick wash-up to his body, washing his face, and brushing his teeth he proceeded to his basement for his daily workout routine. He worked out every morning for at least two hours. He hit the weight bench, did some pushups, and did some sit-ups. When he was done with that he boxed around with his boxing bag, speed bag, and did some shadow boxing. He concluded his workout routine with some Martial Arts moves. After his workout Legend headed up the basement stairs stopping in the kitchen grabbing him a protein shake out of the fridge. Once he finished his shake he went to take a much needed shower.

Standing in the shower he pressed his hands on the tile of the shower walls, held his head down, and enjoyed the feeling of the warm water running down his body. As the water soothed him his mind drifted to his parents thinking of how much he missed them.

His mother Doncia Brunilda Castillo, family sent her to the States when she was eighteen years old so that she could receive a college education. But once she reached Cleveland, Ohio she immediately met and fell in love with his father Gerald Nelson mainly known as G, an up and coming hustler.

When her family back home learned of the love affair between the two, they were mortified. Her father wanted his oldest child to fall in love and marry a man from her own country, the Dominican Republic. But Doncia was very strong willed, stubborn, and was also helplessly in love with the hustler G that her family finally accepted the two. But their union had conditions. Gerald had to marry the young Doncia, which was nothing for him because he was also helplessly in love with her.

Once married, G realized that the marriage had special perks that came along with it; seeing as though her family was the head of the Dominican Drug Cartel. Gerald went from an up and coming hustler to Boss status. He didn't just supply his city; he supplied all of Ohio's major cities Akron, Dayton, Columbus, Cincinnati, Youngstown, and Toledo.

Even though Gerald was a big time Drug dealer, he never wanted his only child to be raised sheltered and secluded. That's why even though he was a Boss, from the outside looking in his family lived a normal middle class family lifestyle. They lived in the Wade Park area of Cleveland in what was considered a mini mansion. They did drive luxury cars but nothing over extravagant. Legend attended public schools where he made friends and he was enrolled in Martial Arts classes where he also made friends. But he was taught at a young age that where his family lay their head and what they had wasn't any ones business. His father never did hide anything about his business from him because he knew one day Legend would be That Nigga.

Unfortunately his father died in a car accident when he was sixteen years old, but in Legend's heart he knew the car crash wasn't an accident at all. He knew his father would have never lost control of the car, even if it was a bad thunder storm that night. So something about the car crash was definitely wrong to him.

After his father passed away, Legend left the States with his mother and his grandparents moving to the Dominican Republic for the rest of his teenage years. He returned to Cleveland at eighteen now knowing even more about the dope game. And with his Dominican half being his supplier he knew he was going to hold Cleveland down providing them with Grade A quality Cocaine, just like his father.

Legend ended his shower and his thoughts. At twenty five he has never felt so alone. Even though he was a private person he was never private with his mother, his father and his good friend Mo Money, who he hasn't seen in over nine years. Yeah he had bitches he fucked and niggas he kicked it with every once in a while, but he never got to close to anyone. He knew letting too many people in his circle could be a potential down fall. So he really didn't have much of a personal life, everything was strictly business.

THREE

Horace kept an apartment on the outskirts of the city which was used for one thing and one thing only. Storing, cooking, and packaging his dope. No one knew of the spot except for Tamia, his cook. She could come and go as she very well pleased.

Tamia had been cooking Horace's product for him since she was about eighteen years old. Her father had taught her the science of cooking dope when she was fifteen. Her father Larry Travis aka Top Dolla was a well-known player in the drug game. And he made sure his daughter knew everything about the game as well. Yes he made sure she went to school getting her book knowledge, but when she came home her street schooling began. He never knew which path she would take so he wanted her prepared for both. Dolla caught a federal case and had been sentence to twenty years when she was seventeen. Now at twenty four she was still putting what she learned into practice.

Horace sat at the dining room table getting his order ready and waiting for Mia to arrive. He looked up from the table when he heard her keys jiggling in the door.

Mia walked through the door a little shocked to see him sitting there. "What's good Horace? I didn't know you would still be here?" She stated after entering the apartment closing and locking the door behind her.

"Yeah I know, but I was running a little behind schedule this morning."

She walked toward the table setting her Gucci bag in the chair, "Okay, so what you got for me?"

He looked up at her beautiful face admiring what he saw. Tamia was a five-seven natural beau. Everything about her was natural from her low haircut to her caramel brown round face, which she wouldn't dare put make-up on, to her pretty manicured finger nails with only clear polish, all put together on a thick 175lb frame. And not to mention her natural breast and ass, any nigga could tell all her shit was home grown, wasn't anything fake about her 36DDDs and her small waist with big hips and wide ass. Tamia was enough to make any grown man have wet dream at least once when they saw her. "Always ready to get down to business uh?"

"That's why I'm here isn't it?"

He stared at her awhile longer, wanting to ask her some questions, but thought against it. So he stood up ready to get down to business. I want five of them in eighths, two in ounces, one in halves, one in quarters, and one in eight balls.

"Okay, I got you boss man." Tamia responded getting her tools ready for work.

Horace chilled for a while sitting on the couch while she worked which kind of threw Mia off. He has never been there when she arrived, during, or after she left.

Usually she came in, went for the work order, did her job, picked up the City Blue bag which contained her payment in a shoe box, locked up and left.

She was trying to pretend he wasn't there but it wasn't working, so she looked up from the package in front of her. "Is everything cool with you? This isn't like you to be here. Is there anything going on?"

"Everything good, just didn't feel like driving right away. A nigga a little tired. You feel me?"

"A'ight. Just checking on you."

He thought he would get an idea of where her head was. He has never seen her with a dude claiming to be her man. Only person he has ever saw her kickin' it with was her girl Shauntille. But he damn sure didn't think they were gay because her girl was fucking his nigga Quan.

"Oh yeah Mia, I meant to tell you, my dude asked about you. He saw you when we were talking the other night outside of the Cocktale."

She looked over at him wondering where the conversation was coming from, they normally only discussed business.

He stood and walked into the kitchen. "Do you think you would like to meet him?"

"Nawl, I'm good. I don't even know who (him) is."

"Oh my bad, it's my dude Legend. We went to elementary school together. I know you have heard of him before? He's the one I get all my work from."

She kept working not wanting the conversation. "I can't say that I have. But let me get back to work. I still got five more pies to bake."

Horace was glad to know that she didn't know Legend and wasn't interested in knowing him either so he walked back over to the couch and gathered his things. He told Mia he would let her handle her business and would get out of her hair.

Tamia took care of her business taking one break in between eating her some food and taking a short nap. When she was finished with everything she stacked the finished product into the safe where she would have got the bricks from if Horace wasn't there in the first place. On the way out of the door she grabbed the City Blue bag that contained her funds and locked up Horace's apartment. She hopped in her 2011 Ford Taurus SEL and headed back to the heart of the city. All she wanted to do now was to take a shower and get some rest. Cooking all that dope took an entire day, literally a whole twenty two hours. Cooking dope was a draining task but the money that she made was so worth it.

FOUR

Legend sat in front of a single family house in Shaker Heights dialing his little freak Charmaine's number.

"Hello," she answered.

"What's good wit' you?"

"Missing you," She responded happy to hear his voice.

"Yeah, is that right? What you doing?"

"Nothing, was about to get ready to cook some lunch."

"You cooking for yourself or yo' company?"

"If that's your way of asking is someone here, it isn't. And if you're on your way I will be cooking for the both of us."

He knew she didn't have anyone there. He knew he was the only person that she wanted in her presence. But one could never be too sure. In his book females were to fickle, they never knew what they really wanted. "I'm outside open the door."

As soon as he walked through the door she threw her arms around him. He hadn't shown his face or even called for two weeks and she missed him something terrible. Not seeing or hearing from him meant nothing to her. She was in love with him and would always be waiting whenever he did decide to surface.

Charmaine met Legend when she was nineteen years old working in a gift shop at the Cleveland Hopkins

Airport and he had just come back to the States. When she first laid eyes on him she knew she was in love, his bald head, his caramel brown skin, his piercing small brown bedroom eyes and his small juicy suckable lips. Not to mention his body. When she saw his five-ten 190lb frame step off the plane she was in heaven. His body was slim but had a lot of cockiness to it. She could tell he was one of them guys that worked out every day. And then his sexy as walk, his swag alone screamed that he was the shit. Now seven years later all she has ever been to him was his friend/fuck partner. But she was content with their arrangement because even though she wasn't his woman he has always treated her with respect. He helped pay her bills every month and made sure she didn't want for anything. And if he did have other bitches she didn't know about them. She has never saw him out with anyone nor has anyone called her phone or came by her house disrespecting her. She just figured he was a private person and she was as close as he was ever going to get to a relationship. Therefore she accepted her position in his life and made sure he was the only man in hers. In her heart she believed when he did get ready to settle down, it would be with her.

After letting him get settled in and giving him the updates of the past two weeks about her job and school she finally made it to the kitchen to fix their lunch. Since he stopped by she decided to make his favorite, a fish boy. Before she got with Legend she had never even heard of the famous fish boy so he had to explain to her that it was just like a polish boy but had fish and cheese on it instead of the polish sausage. When she cooked and tried it, it became her favorite also.

Once they finished with their food Legend did his famous one two, went straight to her bedroom took off every piece of clothing he had on and went straight to sleep. Charmaine on the other hand didn't want him sleep she wanted him inside of her. Hell it had been two whole damn weeks. But looking at him sleep so peaceful she couldn't deny him of his rest. So she decided to clean their lunch dishes, straighten up the house, take a shower, and lay down along side of him.

Legend woke up from his sleep not believing that he was down for three whole hours. He glanced over at Charmaine and saw she was out like a light her damn self. As he looked at her sleep he admired everything about her. She was a gorgeous red bone with long thick jet black hair that she kept looking tight. Her body was amazing, only standing at five feet three inches tall and weighing no more than 135lbs with most of her weight sitting in her tight firm ass. He loved the fact that she worked and was going to school furthering her education. And her house and cooking skills screamed wifey material but for some reason he couldn't take that extra leap with her. He couldn't understand what it was that wouldn't allow him make her his woman. Shit as he thought about it he had never had a woman. He had plenty of bitches that he ran through but none of them stood out enough to become his bottom bitch. But he could say that Charmaine has been the closest thing he has ever had to a main. The others he did just stick and move but he was a little more comfortable around her. After looking her over for about another five minutes he felt that four days was long enough to have gone without any pussy.

She was lying peacefully on her side when she felt Legend slide behind her hugging her around her waist then placing soft kisses on her right shoulder. He slid his hand down her thigh pushing it back towards him just a little so he could get some easy access. He then slid his hand over her mound guiding his index finger between her pussy lips onto her clit. She shuddered the moment his finger touched her clit. And her pussy was already nice and wet for him. She had already pleasured herself when she first lied down beside him. There was no way she could have fallen asleep with the way her pussy was jumping because of his presence.

He whispered in her ear, while circling his finger around her wet clit slowly, "Mmmm, I see you already got her together for me Char. You were missing me that much?"

She started rolling her hips in slow circles to match his pace, "You know we missed you, two weeks is definitely too long. You can't keep doing us like this Legend," she said moaning a little louder as he added pressure to her clit.

He knew she was about to get in her feelings and that was the last thing he wanted. He knew he was going over to her house to get him a good meal, a nap, and some good pussy. Not a discussion about how he treats her and her "kitty cat" as she calls it. Now she just blew whatever foreplay he had planned for her out the window.

Never responding to her comment he stopped playing with her clit, rolled her all the way over on her back, reached across her to the night stand, and grabbed a condom. He sat back on his knees between her petite thighs, opened the condom and slid it on his dick. He then lay on top of her, guiding his dick to her pussy hole, then pushing all his thick nine inches deep inside of her.

He rocked her body to a steady beat with her moaning and crying the entire time about how much she loved him, how much she needed him permanently, and then begging him not to go so deep because she couldn't handle all of him.

He eased up positioning himself where he could stare in her teary eyes, the whole while thinking how she could want to be his when she couldn't even handle his dick. It had been seven fucking years and she still wasn't used to him yet. By now she should be grabbing his ass begging for him to go deeper and begging for him to hit it harder. And at that moment while staring in her eyes he saw that she really was in pain. So he eased up some more and went a little slower. Now he realized what it was that was keeping her from being his main.

How was she going to be his woman and couldn't handle his dick. He knew while he was grinding in her at a slow pace she was in heaven believing they were making love. But to him he was just getting the feel of some good pussy and trying to accommodate her at the same time because that's all she could handle. And on top of that she was a complete square. Which was cool at times, but not as his woman. She wouldn't be able to handle his lifestyle if she knew the real. She would probably worry herself crazy if she knew all the risk he took on a daily basis. So no she could never be his bottom bitch. His woman needed to be just like him, educated and understood the rise and the fall of the drug game.

Legend kept grinding slowly in and out of her until he felt her cum on his dick. He pushed off of her lying down and pulling off his condom. He then guided her head to his dick "suck me 'til I bust and you better not stop 'til you've swallowed every last drop."

Charmaine obeyed his every command.

FIVE

Tamia ran inside the Salvation Army thrift store on Turney Road in Garfield Hts. looking for some more Pyrex Vision pots, with her best friend Shauntille. She hated that the company had stop making the glassware in pots. Now that was all available in retail stores were like the baking dishes for the oven, which was the reason why she always had to go to thrift stores hoping she found what she really needed. She knew the government had something to do with them not making the pots anymore knowing that's what people used to cook their dope in. Motherfuckers!

As she scanned the houseware aisle her phone started vibrating. She looked at the caller ID noticing it was her father's cell number. Yeah he was on a Federal Penitentiary Camp but her daddy was the man, he kept him a cell phone at all times. As she bent down to get a good look on the bottom shelf she handed her phone to her best friend so she could answer.

"Hey Top", Shauntille said into the phone.

"You better stop playing wit' me Shaunie girl, what I tell you about that? You're my daughter too."

Shaunie did her usual laugh with her big smile on her face, "Hey Dad".

"That's better, so what my girls doing?"

"We're doing a little shopping at the thrift store for the old lady that lives next door to Mia."

Top knew Mia wasn't shopping for an old lady, he knew exactly what his baby girl was shopping for. "Okay, tell her I need for her to do some shopping for me too and I need y'all down here this weekend. I'll call later with my list."

"Okay, I'll make sure I tell her and of course we'll be there."

"Alright Shaunie girl, I'll talk to y'all later."

"K"

Shauntille handed Tamia back her phone and relayed her father's message to her.

Tamia nodded her head and headed to the front counter after finding exactly what she needed. She loved the thrift store. She guessed the government didn't realize that elderly people were going to upgrade their cookware and donate their older ones. That was a plus for her.

After leaving the thrift store Tamia called her dad back to get his order.

"Hey Baby Girl, did you find what your neighbor needed?"

"Yeah I did Daddy. What's up wit' you, what do you need me to pick up?"

Her father gave her a list of name brand tennis shoes, T-shirts, socks, boxer briefs, and jogging suits all in different sizes. He also gave her a food, cigarette, liquor, and even a weed list. He wanted some regular and some loud. All going to cost her well over a thousand dollars, but it was cool because she knew he was going to make over three thousand when he finished selling the items.

Her father was a hustler and a Federal Penitentiary Camp wasn't going to stop his action. Top Dolla got money when he was on the streets and he made damn sure he got his fair share off the streets. Hell he even got pussy on the weekends. Females would go down get a room and inmates would sneak off the camp, get them some pussy then head back before anyone knew they were gone.

All of these activities under Top's command, she smiled thinking *how much her Daddy was a certified Hustler.*

"Alright Daddy I got you, we'll be down this weekend."

"Thanks Mia. And did John's girl send that money to that Rush Card?"

"Yup, Shaunie told me it was loaded on their last night."

"Okay Baby, Daddy loves you and will talk to you later, make sure you be safe."

"K, Daddy, love you too."

BOSSES

Legend family owned a chain of Self Storage Facilities in most of the Cleveland Suburb areas. They were located in Cleveland Heights, Warrensville Heights, Shaker Heights, Bedford Heights, Garfield Heights, Maple Heights, Down Town Cleveland and they even had some out in Twinsburg and Macedonia. They were quiet places of business. Most people who stored their things there checked on their units every once in a while or as needed because the company owner's kept the facilities heavy with security. So they knew their valuables were safe.

Even he owned a dummy account in every facility. The accounts held both a male and a female name on them as if the units were being rented by couples.

He sat in the office of the Storage Facility in Maple Heights with his Uncle Victor looking at the security monitor. They watched as the sophisticated Continental Stewardess in her mid-twenties went to her a storage unit looking like she must have been coming straight from the Airport. She stayed inside her unit for all of fifteen minutes. They watched as she pulled down the storage unit door locked it and rolled her suitcase to her car. She put her suitcase in her trunk, jumped in her car, through her Steve Madden aviator sunglasses on her face and drove to the gate so she could let herself out. Legend smiled knowing the suitcase contained Quan's usual fifteen bricks and when the Continental Stewardess returned in two days her suitcase would contain his usual $375,000 that she would put in the storage unit, lock it up and head back to the Airport for her five days of work, traveling to wherever Continental took her.

After he left the Storage Facility he decided he would run up to The Hair Chamber on Northfield Road so his boy TC could give him a fresh shave to his head and low trim to his beard, seeing as though he was already near Bedford. But before he made that stop he wanted to run inside Wal-Mart to get him some hygiene items. While inside Wal-Mart he gave Charmaine a call to see if she needed some things at her house. Even though he knew she was never going to be his main he felt she was still a good person at heart and he would always look out for her.

Once Charmaine heard Legend's special ring tone she damn near broke her neck trying to answer.

"Hey Baby"

"What's good Char? What you doing?"

"Nothing just got off work about to head down to Cleveland State to my Psychology class. Why, what you doing?"

"I'm in Wal-Mart doing some hygiene shopping and wanted to know did you need some things."

"Baby you must have read my mind. I was going to go after my class but since you're already there it's perfect."

"Okay, shoot wit yo' list."

As she went on with her list someone caught his eye. A female smiling and waving at him. As a matter a fact it was one Quan's girls. As he ended his call the female started walking over towards him.

She walked over to him giving him a slight hug, "Hey Legend, how you doing, haven't seen you in a while."

"Yeah I have been busy taking care of business. How about you? You been good?"

"As good as I can be."

He looked in her shopping cart and saw a lot of male items inside. "What you doing some shopping for Quan?"

"Um, no, I'm mad at him right now. My best friend and I are picking up some stuff for her Dad."

"Where is your best friend?" He asked looking around because he didn't see her standing with anyone.

"She's on the grocery side. We split the list because we didn't want to be in here all day."

"That's cool. Well it was good seeing you Shauntille."

"You to Legend", she responded waving bye and walking off towards the checkout lines.

Legend finished his shopping then headed to the checkout counter. After he finished placing all of his items on the belt he noticed Shauntille walking out of the store with none other than the mysterious Mia, again only seeing the back of her head but now knew her body from anywhere. *Okay I see you Miss Mia.*

SIX

Tamia and Shauntille jumped on the highway heading to I-70W for the six and half hour drive to Terri Haute, Indiana. Tamia hated the long drive but with her best friend by her side it didn't seem so bad.

Tamia met her best friend of the past seven years when she was seventeen and her father had just been sentenced to do his jail bid. She had to go pick up some money from one of her father's lil dudes that owed him a couple of dollars. But instead of his dude Tim meeting up with her he sent his girl Shauntille. After a couple of meetings at the mall with Mia picking up money from Shauntille, they started shopping together and the two quickly grew to like one another. After Tim caught a federal case having to do a little time, Tamia and Shauntille stayed in touch with one another and became the best of friends despite the fact that they were complete opposites. Tamia was more of the tomboy girlie type and Shauntille being the girlie girl bougie type.

They did kind of ran around the same circle of niggas. Shauntille keeping a couple dope boys in her pocket and Tamia cooking for a couple of dope boys. But never did their niggas cross, if Shaunie was fucking a nigga Mia didn't cook for them. She didn't like mixing the two. For one she didn't need her business all over the place and for two she didn't want any problems when Shaunie got through with a dude and Mia was still handling business with him. She didn't need any crazy nigga she was doing business with in her ear worrying about her best friend or no crazy nigga trying to kill her best friend, all because they were going through pussy withdrawal.

Shauntille's current dope boy flavor was Quan. She and Quan had been kicking it off and on for the past three years. More so on than off. Out of all the niggas she fucked with none of them made her feel the way Quan did. In her heart they were the perfect match. Everything about him turned her on. His 210lbs fitted his six-one height perfectly, his caramel skin that seemed to match his light brown eyes, his juicy lips that covered a perfect set of white teeth, and what she loved the most was his dread locks that he kept pulled to the back ever so neatly. And not to mention there wasn't a stingy bone in his body. If she asked she received. His only down fall was he still had to many females in his stable. He claims they only do business for him. Tamia told her that could be the absolute truth, but Shauntille knew he was still fucking most of them.

The two made it to Terri Haute safely around eight that night with only making two stops. They checked into the Drury Inn and chilled waiting for that important phone call that they knew they were going to receive bright and early in the morning.

Tamia took off her clothes and headed straight to the shower. After she was done Shauntille jumped in. While Shaunie was in the shower Mia decided to call her Terri Haute action.

"I hope you're calling to tell me that you're around my parts", Ant said as soon as he answered his phone.

"Yeah I am. I'm at the Drury Inn so grab us a room here when you got time, you know I got to be up and out by six in the morn."

"That's what's up. I'll text you the room number in a minute."

"K"

When Shauntille emerged from the bathroom and saw Mia getting off her cell she knew exactly who she was talking to.

"I don't even need to ask what you're about to get into."

"Nope, you sure don't."

Tamia headed to the room number that Ant texted to her phone and gave the door a slight tap. He snatched the door open and yanked her inside. He hugged her tight while kissing the side of her neck and pressing her body against the door, smothering the hell out of her. Mia nipped his shoulder with her teeth hoping that would have him ease up a little. When he finally decided to give her a little breathing room he stared into her eyes and she saw that look that lets her know he missed the hell out of her.

There was no describing Ant besides the fact he was a baldhead chocolate Mandingo God with a big ass dick. And that was all she wanted from him, his big ass dick that she loved to ride. Mia stepped away from him looking his body over. She loved the fact that he wasn't wearing anything but a dry towel around his waist. She smiled thinking *he knows exactly what I want*. She started backing him up towards the bed and once he couldn't go back any further she opened his towel letting it drop to the floor and pushed him down. She stood in front of him pulling her Victoria's Secret tank above her head and sliding the matching boy shorts to the floor. She straddled his body and crawled up towards his face. With her knees on both sides of his head she spread her pussy lips open and lowered her clit directly over his mouth. There were no words needed, she knew what she wanted and so did he. Ant grabbed a hold of her thighs so he could hold her in place because he was about to eat her pussy until she begged him to let the muthafucka go. He didn't tease her pussy; he knew that wasn't what she wanted. So he clasped his lips around her clit and began to suck very slowly. He let her clit go and began to lick in fast circles.

She didn't know if she was coming or going. She loved the way Ant ate her pussy, the nigga had a Tornado tongue. "Yes... Right there Ant... Yes... Please don't stop." She moaned as she continued to spread her lips for him.

He started swirling his tongue around even faster and then she started cumming and bucking all over his face. "Yes... Ant...damn..." He never let her thighs go after she recovered, he just watched as her clit jumped up and down begging for more. He couldn't deny the most beautiful and fattest clit, so he clasped he lips around it once again and started sucking it nice and slow. He knew she preferred him to suck fast, but he knew her pussy and body better than she thought he did. When he sucked nice and slow her pussy would bless him with the creamiest nectar and she would start hollering and swearing to the Lord Himself. And as he kept sucking that's exactly what happened, her creamy juices slid down his throat as she hollered "Oh... My... Muthafuckin'... God..."

When she came down off her high she slid herself down his body until her thighs were straddled over his and reached her hand out for him to pass her a condom. After she placed the condom on his dick she eased her pussy down his long, thick, juicy pole, and started riding him nice and slow then hard and fast.

His dick was so big so she always rode him. She needed to be in control with how much pain she was willing to endure. She wasn't going to let any nigga pound in and out of her pussy fucking her shit up.

She kept with his pace bringing her pussy to the tip and sliding down real slow. She rode him like that until they both were cumming, hollering, and swearing to the Lord together.

She rolled off of his dick lying beside him, with him pulling her into his arms.

"Something gotta give lil mama."

"Something like what?"

"Something like us. I want more Mia and I'm going to have more. Either you're going to relocate here or I'm coming there."

"Not yet Ant, okay."

He got out of bed heading towards the bathroom, "You got sixty days. If you're not here then I'll be there."

With that he went inside the bathroom not even caring if she had a response.

BOSSES

Mia's cell phone rang at 7:30am on the dot.

"Y'all ready to rock and roll?" Top asked his daughter.

"Always"

Mia and Shauntille already had their things in the trunk of the car and her Dad's duffle bags inside big black garbage bags on the back seat of the car. Shauntille talked to Top and one of his dudes that was out in the field doing yard work on the phone as Mia drove down the long road towards the prison's camp grounds. As they drove they could see the prisoners out on the federal grounds without a fence doing their Saturday morning chores. As they started getting close to their drop off spot Top's dude asked, "This y'all in this white Cavalier?"

"Yeah", Shauntille replied.

"Alright tell her to pull in by the little cottage."

Tamia turned the car into the driveway of the cottage and before she could even put her foot on the brakes good two big niggas opened both of the back car doors, pulled out the garbage bags, slammed the doors, put the bags on the back of the pick-up truck and went back to work like nothing ever happened. Mia threw the car in reverse as soon as the doors shut and headed back to the long road, with her and Shaunie on their way back to the highway for their six and half hour drive back to The Land.

SEVEN

Legend met up with Quan for lunch at Lancers to discuss a little business and to get them some good seafood. Lancers Scampi was to die for.

When Quan walked through the door Legend admired his nigga. He rocked a white POLO shirt with the beige POLO symbol, some khaki POLO Cargo shorts, with a pair of POLO RALPH LAUREN Bienne Boat Shoes. His dreads were neat as always, but what he didn't have on was his big dumb ass diamond earrings. His arm was draped with a Franck Muller watch but not one that was to flashy, he rocked an 8885 C CC DT from the CASABLANCA Collection.

Quan greeted him with their normal nod and dap as he sat down at the table.

"I see you my nigga. I told you, you didn't need all that flossy shit to look fly." Legend smiled as he schooled his friend.

"Yeah, you were right L. I done fucked around and caught a punk ass weed case, but what caught their attention was the bling."

Legend's smile left his face. "You caught a case? When nigga? And when the fuck was you going to tell me?" He asked as he bombarded him with questions.

"Nigga I just told you. And they didn't get shit off me but a punk ass quarter bag of loud. You know I don't ride around dirty. They did call themselves taking my jewelry and watch but I got that shit right back."

"How you get it back?" He asked looking at Quan sideways.

"L, I know you think I don't know what the fuck I'm doing, but nigga I ain't stupid. When I got all the jewelry I had my lil paralegal broad pay for them with her credit card, which she still paying monthly payments on. But I did give her the cash up front and the shit wasn't bought at one time. They were bought around Christmas and my birthday. So she told them they were gifts and she showed them her receipts and credit card statements. And to add insult to injury she showed them her check stubs letting them muthafucka's know she could afford it. They gave me my shit right back."

"My nigga, a nigga apologize for doubting you my man; I didn't know you were on top of your game like that."

"It's cool man. You didn't know because all I have ever shown you outside of our business side was the young and wild shit I be doing."

They stop talking when the waitress approached the table to take their order. They ordered their meals and sent the waitress on her way.

Legend picked right up with their conversation, "I didn't know you had a paralegal under your belt. That's a good thing, which lawyer she works for?"

"Nigga Boss Lawyers, some Italians Downtown in the Arcade, and you do know my girl Shauntille."

"I didn't know she was a paralegal, that's good that you keep a square. But I just saw her the other day at Wal-Mart. She was with the same girl I asked Horace about.

Female named Mia." Legend asked hoping he could get some leads on the Miss Mia.

"Yeah she a square alright but her ass is always trying to stomp with the big dogs. But her girl Mia on the other hand is far from a square, and she works as a paralegal also for the same Italians, but she ain't into it like Shauntille. My girl works every day, Mia just do it when they really need her. They hired them both as a favor to Mia's father, but as it turns out their excellent at what they do. Shauntille actually going to start law school this fall and Mia is going to be her paralegal."

"Why her girl ain't going go to law school with her?"

"Mia likes to be behind the scenes, hence the very reason why you saw her wit Horace."

"Yeah, he told me she's his cook."

"A very good cook at that, Horace said she charges niggas a stack per pie if you got 15 or more, but if you got less than 15 the charge is 1,250. Her ass won't cook shit for me though. Talking 'bout she don't like crossing lines seeing as though I'm fuckin' wit' her girl, she don't want shit to feel awkward when me and ole girl through. Hell I've been fucking wit' Shaunie for the past three years now. She about her business so why the fuck will I fuck that up?"

"Damn, lil mama making a killing then. Shit Horace gets twenty of them thangs from me about every two weeks. Not to mention you say he ain't the only nigga that she cooks for. Shit if I was her I would only do that paralegal shit as needed too. Getting it like that from behind the scenes. And for real my nigga you got to respect her policy, she probably doesn't want you going psycho on her girl and y'all still handling business."

"Yeah you right and she's cool peoples too, she's the one that suggested to me that I put my shit in Shaunie's name. I guess she knows how her girl feels about me, so she was looking out, puttin' a nigga up on his game."

"That's what's up. But now what I really want to know, who is her dad? Got Italians doing favors for him?" Legend asked right as the waitress approached with their food. And once again when she left they were back to politicing.

"I don't know much about her dad but that he was a get money nigga and now he's doing a bid in the federal pen."

"Okay, when I saw Shauntille at Wal-Mart she said they were doing some shopping for her girl's father. Is he on his way home?"

Quan gave his nigga a slight smile, "Nawl my nigga they probably was going to do a drop down at the camp. I told you she was far from a square."

He gave him a questioning look so Quan proceeded to tell him how the drop went.

I don't understand my nigga, the way you talking, it seems like you're cool wit Mia too. Seeing as though you know all her info so cooking for you shouldn't be a problem."

"I know all that from pillow talking, as for the cooking I got that info from Horace, I'm pretty sure Mia doesn't know I know some of her other shit like that."

Legend started to dig in his food. He looked up at Quan stating, "You better stop her from that pillow talk shit, you don't want her pillow talkin' wit' another nigga about your ass. You feel me?"

"Yeah I feel you, but she ain't like that, she confided in me because I started questioning why she was taking so many trips. You know it was either one or two things, they were meeting niggas to fuck or they were fucking each other. That's when she told me the truth but she also told me her girl does have a nigga down there she fucking but wants me to believe that she don't, yeah whatever. But anyway nigga I know you don't go out and all but I know you're going to show your face at The Legacy Lounge this Friday for my birthday. Right?"

"Yeah I'll be there." He replied hoping he would run into Mia there. Talking to Quan had him past intrigued.

They finished their food then left going their separate ways. Also with Legend not even mentioning the opportunity he had for Quan to make some more money. He told himself he had to do some investigating about that case shit. He needed to make sure weed was all it was about. And his mind was on Mia. If she's getting money like that, he knows some young niggas is going to try her. And he definitely doesn't want that to happen, just hearing of her she sounds like good peoples.

Smiling to himself *shit ole girl cooking pies, taking risk for her pops, and into that legal shit, now that's what I'm talking about. Miss Mia a muthafuckin' Boss!*

EIGHT

Shauntille finally convinced Tamia to step out and have a couple of drinks with her for Quan's birthday even though she was still mad at him. By the time she reached Mia's door she was ready to go and get her party on but of course her best friend wasn't ready, coming to the door with just her bra and panties on.

"Girl, why the hell you ain't ready?" She fumed at her friend.

"Because I didn't know what the atmosphere was going to be and you didn't give me the run down on the dress code." Mia responded as she walked her thick ass up the stairs to her bedroom with Shaunie in tow.

"Like you really care if I give you the dress code, you're going to do the exact opposite anyway. So I figured I'll let you do you."

As they walked in her bedroom she turned on her heels, "You're absolutely right. So it's only going to take me a second, but look at you. Looking like it's your birthday and not your mans."

Shauntille's body was laced in a black Dolce&Gabbana Ruched Satin Dress complementing her 125lb five-one frame. Draping her neck was a black Vera Wang Crystal Bib Necklace. Her size seven feet were snuggled in a pair of Champaign colored Croc-Sequined Peep-toe Platform Pumps by Christian Louboutin with a black Prada Turnlock Continental Ruched Wallet nestled in her small fresh manicured fingers. She had her hair flat ironed boned straight with a part in the middle. And her MAC makeup was flawless shadowing her oval shaped face.

"This is nothing, it's what lies beneath. That's where the true prize is." Shaunie stated as she pulled the strap of her dress over her shoulder a tad bit.

"I know you're rocking that La Perla underneath. Quan is going to be one happy birthday boy." Mia replied as she trailed her finger down Shauntille's bra strap. She removed her hand and began to walk away, "Now let me go put something together real quick."

Shauntille stopped her by grabbing her arm with her left hand. She then guided her right hand to Tamia's pussy, "After I make you cum first."

"Come on now Shaunie, do you want to be late to yo' man's party?" Mia moaned as Shauntille slid her hand in her panties and began to rub her clit.

Shauntille circled her middle finger around Mia's clit, "This won't take long. Look how wet and fat your clit is, she already about to explode."

"Ooh…Shaunie…just like that," Mia moaned as she placed her hand on top of Shauntille's.

She pushed Mia's hand away, "I don't need any help. Don't anybody know this pussy better than I do." Shauntille said as she rubbed her pussy in slight slow circles.

Tamia always loved the way Shauntille made her pussy feel. She twirled her hips to match the pace of Shaunie's fingers. "Yes…just like that…you're right…don't nobody know this pussy like you…yes…Shaunie damn."

Shauntille gripped Mia's hip and began to circle her clit faster with more pressure, "Cum for me Mia," She whispered.

Tamia gripped Shauntille's head rubbing her hands through her soft long hair then pressed her lips against Shaunie's.

Shauntille slid her tongue in Mia's mouth, "Cum for me Mia," She whispered once more.

On cue Mia's body shook as her pussy blessed her best friend's fingers, "Oh my God...Shaunie...Oh my God." Mia kept kissing Shauntille biting her juicy bottom lip slightly as she came down off her climax.

Shauntille continued to lightly stroke Mia's clit 'til she knew her climax subsided. Once she was satisfied she pulled her hand out of Mia's panties then slapped her on her ass, "Now hurry up and get yourself together so we can go."

Mia stood there still dazed from the pleasure her best friend had given her. "What about you?"

Shauntille walked towards the bathroom to wash her hands and to fix her hair and face, "I'm good, seeing you tremble like a baby has me nice and wet for Quan."

"What the hell eva," Tamia said then followed behind her best friend so she could wash her pussy.

When she was done cleaning herself she waltzed her thick naked behind into her walk-in closet then waltzed out wearing an Eileen Fisher white Linen Tank Jersey with the matching Linen Cargo Pants. She stood in front of her mirror and laced her neck with an 18K gold Snake Necklace by Aurelie Bidermann with the matching Snake

Cuff circling her left wrist. She threw her Gurham Amulet 24K Gold and Silver stud earrings in her ear and gave her short haircut one last brush over then glossed her thin lips with her MAC clear lip gloss. She then waltzed back into her walk-in closet and sashayed out with her Christian Louboutin Gold Maggie Glitter & Snake Platform Pumps on her feet and with her Judith Leiber Python & Pave Crystal Clutch in her hand.

Shauntille walked up to her best friend tapped her on her ass telling her "now let's go thickness."

As soon as they walked through the Legacy doors Quan scooped Shaunie in his arms.

"I was hoping you came. And tonight is the night we call a truce because you're leaving wit' me. Right?" He asked as he tilted her head back and gave her a gentle kiss on the lips. When they separated Shaunie answered, "Right."

When he noticed Mia standing behind Shauntille he gave her a wide smile. He let go of his boo and held out his hand to give Mia some dap. "The sky must be about to fall if Shaunie got you to come outside to play tonight."

"Whatever playboy," she responded pushing his hand away and embracing him with a hug, "Happy Birthday."

He thanked her then went to release their hug but she held on to him tighter whispering in his ear, "You know my girl love you, so I'm advising you not to mistreat her."

After giving Quan a gentle warning she sashayed herself over to the bar and ordered a Ciroc coconut with pineapple juice and a splash of cranberry juice on the rocks. While sitting on the bar stool she surveyed her surroundings digging the atmosphere in the spot. The Club had a kind of Gothic feel to it but a Sexy Gothic, with a black and gold and a pinch of red color scheme. The décor looked like whoever decorated it tipped on the edge of the darkness just a little bit.

She noticed that one of the booths were empty so that's where she decided to parlay for the rest of the night, towards the front of the bar with easy access to an exit and with her back against the wall. By the time Shaunie and Quan had joined her she was well into her third drink and second glass of ice water. She excused herself from the table letting them know she was going to the ladies room.

Horace and Legend had arrived at the bar at the same time. Of course Horace pulled up in a white Range Rover sitting on 23's. Legend just shook his head thinking how niggas be wearing and driving that flossy shit putting a target on their back. Legend on the other hand kept it simple stepping out of a 2012 Tuxedo Black LINCOLN MKS with Charcoal Interior. He smiled to himself about his car, yeah it was a nice ass car but he didn't have it piped out, he kept it sexy the way the designer intended it to be.

When the two entered the bar Quan stood to greet them with some dap as they approached the booth. "My nigga Legend made it out, thanks man. I think the sky really is going to fall tonight. "Quan boasted as he looked up at the ceiling.

"Boy sit yo' tipsy self down, keep telling people the sky go' fall," Shaunie stated standing giving both men hugs and explaining how her best friend came and how Quan told her the very same thing.

Horace immediately started looking around trying to see if he could spot Mia. He hasn't seen her in a couple of weeks since he didn't want her to feel funny if he was at the spot all of a sudden when she came to take care of business. It would have been out of their normal routine.

Legend being the boss that he is just smiled on the inside thinking he finally would get to meet the infamous Miss Mia.

Tamia headed back to the booth not paying any attention to the numerous guys that were trying to holla at her. There wasn't one nigga in the club that had peaked her interest. They were all too flossy, flamboyant, and seemed to be trying too hard. Flashy cars and outrageous jewelry didn't attract her. She had learned as a young girl that real G's moved in silence. Her father had taught her that it could be fifty balling ass niggas in a room but she would be able to decipher which one was the mastermind of the operation. He explained to her how his appearance would be different from the rest, he would stand different from the rest, and when he opened his mouth to speak his speech and vocabulary would definitely set him apart from the rest also.

As she passed by the bar getting closer to the booth she noticed that Horace had arrived. Not really wanting to be in his presence at the moment because of their last awkward encounter she began to turn around to go sit at the bar, but then she noticed the guy standing next to Horace.

Only the back of his smooth baldhead could be seen but there were some things definitely special about the guy. His slim lean muscular body frame for one. He wasn't cock diesel but she could see every well sculpted muscle in his arms and back through the white Embroidered Linen MICHAEL KORS shirt that he was wearing. His long one of a kind slight bow legs for two, which were draped in some Gucci Classic Unwashed jeans. His small head that was now bald for three. She always knew he would probably one day shave his head because he had one of those hairlines that one could tell was going to recede at a young age, just like his father's. And last but not least his beautiful caramel dark skin. It wasn't the typical dark skin that niggas was blessed with, but that smooth caramel/milk chocolate skin that was the result of black and brown relations, that seemed to have been kissed by the island sun. It may have been damn near a decade since she last saw him but she knew exactly who he was, so she made her way over to the group.

Horace was the first to acknowledge Mia's presence. "What's good Mia?"

She didn't even respond to Horace, she just stood directly behind the guy saying, "Lil G."

He couldn't believe his ears, he knew that voice from anywhere and there would only be one person in Cleveland that would call him by that name.

Legend turned only to come face to face with none other than Top Dolla's daughter.

As he looked upon her he could see the ponytails in her hair that she used to wear when she was five years old. He could see the two French braids she used to rock when she was nine. He could also see her with a long wrap at fifteen which was the last time he had seen her. And now here she stood with all her hair chopped off of her head rocking brush waves looking finer than a motherfucker.

"Mo muthafuckin' Money" he finally replied coming out of his trance that she had him captivated in.

She jumped in his arms giving him the biggest hug never wanting to let him go.

They stayed embraced in a silent hug with Shauntille, Quan, and Horace looking at them, then at each other wondering what was going on.

Legend could feel a hole being burned into him by someone so he opened his eyes only to see Horace mean muggin' him. He matched Horace's stare as he spoke in Mia's ear. "Is Horace your man or something?"

Never opening her eyes she replied "No", in the crook of his neck.

Still staring back at Horace he continued in her ear, "Well are you fucking him or something?"

"Hell. No. Why?"

Closing his eyes and hugging his nigga Mo tighter he told her, "no reason."

As Mia basked in being in her lost friend's arms she could now feel someone burning her with their eyes as well. She opened her eyes only to see a pretty petite well-dressed female staring at her with her arms crossed over her chest and tapping her Prada Round Toe Platform Multi Blue Snakeskin Pump, that she had her eye on the other day at the mall, against the floor. Looking the female in the eyes with her mouth still in the crook of Legend's neck she asked him was the female standing behind him his woman.

Legend lifted his head looking over his shoulder and noticed Charmaine standing there with a look on her face he has never seen before. She looked as if she was ready to murder everybody in the spot. He turned his head back around placing it in its original position, "Nah she ain't my woman but she is my girl."

She closed her eyes hugging her friend tighter praying that they would never lose contact again.

Horace was the first to speak getting both Mia's and Legend's attention. "I thought you said you didn't know a guy named Legend, Mia?"

She released her hold on Legend never entertaining the question that Horace had asked her, but she did introduce him to Shaunie as her childhood friend Lil G.

She signaled the waitress over to order a round of drinks. Everyone placed their order but when it was her turn Legend ordered for her, ordering her a ginger-ale along with him. She gave him a look like 'what the hell'.

He ignored the face she was giving him and ushered her to the booth to sit. He bent down and whispered in her ear, "You've already had enough to drink; I can smell it on you." When he went to stand back up he felt someone pressing against him, he turned to see a furious Charmaine.

"What's good Char?"

"What's good? What the fuck you mean what's good? Who the fuck is this bitch you're hugged up on like I, ain't fuckin' here?" Charmaine fused while pointing her finger a little too close to Tamia's face.

Tamia didn't have any words or questions for the female Legend called Char, she knocked her hand out of her face stood and punched her in the face sending her flying into the waitress that was carrying their drinks.

It happen so fast no one saw it coming. Well no one but Shaunie. Once she saw the girl's finger to close for comfort in her girls face she slid over giving Mia some room to steady her feet.

Charmaine went to lunge at Mia once she got over the shock of getting punched and seeing the blood running down the front of her dress from her nose.

Quan jumped up and grabbed Charmaine holding her back. No one dared to attempt to hold Mia, especially not Legend. He looked upon Charmaine like she was a stranger. The drama she was now show casing was a complete 360 from what he was used to, thinking *this dumb bitch has definitely dismissed herself from my life, walking over disrespecting me and cursing at me out the side of her damn neck.*

"Charmaine, man what the fuck is wrong wit' you?" Quan asked.

"Quan get yo' damn hands off me. I'm about to beat this bitch's ass."

"Man Char calm yo' ass down. Why the fuck you over here any damn way, putting your hand in her damn face. You don't even fuckin' know her."

Then he turned his attention to Legend, "She cursing you out questioning you and shit. How the fuck do you even know my cousin?"

"That doesn't matter. Now let me the fuck go." Charmaine fumed at her cousin.

"Char, go sit yo' dramatic ass down somewhere." Quan yelled at her.

The crowd parted as the bouncers finally made it over to their booth. When they noticed Legend standing there they stopped not wanting any problems.

He held up his hand letting the bouncers know everything was cool. He grabbed Tamia by the hand and headed towards the door. He stopped and turned to give Quan his attention, responding to the question he had asked him, "She was cool peoples, one of my fucks, but now she ain't nothing." Then he walked out of the Legacy Lounge just as smooth as he walked in with his nigga Mo Money on his arm.

Charmaine being upset and embarrassed about what Legend had just said directed her attention towards the bouncers. "That bitch snuck and punched me in my face and y'all go' let her leave like ain't shit happen."

Jamie the cockiest bouncer of them all shrugged his shoulders, "What the hell you want us to do, she walking out wit' the boss man," then turned so he could return to his post.

"What the hell he means the boss man?" Charmaine questioned speaking to no one in particular.

The waitress walked past her and Quan telling her, "The boss man as in the owner."

Hearing the news that the waitress had shared shocked Charmaine, Quan, Shauntille, and Horace, but Shaunie was the first to break the silence chuckling, "The Legacy Lounge as in Legend, who would've thought."

NINE

Tamia turned in her seat to get a good look at Legend. She couldn't believe that she was actually with her nigga again. They grew up around each other like every dope family did. Big G was like her uncle and Top Dolla was like Legend's, but now thinking back on it that shit was crazy, because they grew up only knowing each other's nick names. They were together almost every weekend and never knew one another governments. All that time she thought his name was Gerald after his father seeing as though his father and mother were the ones that called him Lil G.

"Okay G, this shit ends today. I know now that your name is Legend but what else goes with it."

He smiled at her, he was thinking the very exact thing. "Legend Alarico Castillo, now what's yours?"

"Tamia Monae Travis"

"Oh so that's where Top got Mo from, your middle name."

"Why did everyone call you Lil G if your name wasn't Gerald and why do you have a Spanish last name if your mother father were married?"

"My mother didn't care for the name Gerald. If you can recall she rarely called him by his name. So she named me Legend saying I was going to be someone great and everyone was going to remember me, but they both still called me Lil G because that's who I was, my father's son. As far as the last name, when my mother married my father she didn't change her last name. She wanted to continue to carry her Dominican father's name, and so will I."

"Your father couldn't have cared for that, most men want their sons to carry their full name. I could understand him agreeing not to name you Gerald, but for you not to have his last name must have hurt."

"It probably did, but I soon realized in their marriage, what my mother said, is the way things went."

For the rest of the ride they both were silent having their own private thoughts. But when he pulled in his drive way she broke that routine. "You have to be kidding me. There's no way you still live in the same house."

"Why not?"

"Because I used to stop by here every weekend for an entire year straight, I gave up thinking there was no way I would catch you here if a year had past."

He opened his car door then walked around to the passenger side to let her out of the car.

"Well you should have kept coming because I moved back in when I came back from the Dominican Republic when I turned eighteen."

She turned to face him, "so that's where you were?"

"Yup, now come on, we can play catch up on the inside."

Tamia felt awkward walking towards Legend's home with him. The last time she was there was when she was fifteen and he had caught her playing with herself. The room she used to sleep in when she was there on the weekends was next to his which was adjoined with a Jack and Jill bathroom. It was nothing for them to share a bathroom. When it was her turn to occupy the space all she had to do was lock the door leading to his room on the inside and vice versa. One night in particular her body was going through some changes. She couldn't understand why her private area was jumping and thumping all around. All she knew was when she placed her hand down there and pressed the flesh in the middle it felt better, hell it actually felt good. So she glanced at the bedroom door making sure it was locked. She then spread her legs open giving her private area some much needed attention that it was requiring. When she pressed the fleshy area in the middle it felt wet and sticky and she started rubbing it in slow circles. It was feeling so good that she dipped her fingers in and out of her hole bringing some more of wetness to the flesh now that felt more like a thick small circle. She was making her private feel so good she got lost with playing with it moaning and rolling her eyes to the back of her head.

Legend stepped through the bathroom door about to tell her something but was stopped abruptly when he saw her pleasuring herself. He was in awe when he saw her face filled with ecstasy. She didn't notice him standing there until she was at the point of no return. When they locked eyes there was no way in hell she was going to stop the feeling that she was giving herself. By them staring in each other's eyes only intensified the sensation she was feeling, which a couple seconds later her legs had stretched out with her making her body cum for the first time. He stared in her eyes and at her pussy while she came loving what he saw. His feet didn't move from the place they were planted in until her breaths slowed and her climax subsided. He then turned going into the bathroom closing the door behind him and jumping in the shower. Inside he jacked his dick off with images of his nigga Mo Money playing with her pussy. He was far from a virgin, shit his dad gave him an entire night with an eighteen year old for his fourteenth birthday. And with all the chicken heads he had at his school he was also far from an amateur but at sixteen years old he had never seen anything as sexy in his life as he did when he was watching Mo.

The next morning her father came to retrieve her bright and early so he could get her to her mother because they were going on their annual trip to Spring Field, Colorado to visit Mia's grandfather for the next three weeks. She didn't get a chance to say goodbye to Lil G because he had already left for his Martial Arts class.

She was only in Colorado for a day before she heard the news of Legend's father. She called to give him her condolences and told him she would be there as soon as she and her mother got off the Amtrak. But when she made it back to Cleveland and to his house he wasn't there. She went to his house every weekend after for a year straight finally giving up thinking she was never going to see her good friend again.

When they entered the house Mia was in amazement, she was greeted by the most beautiful big black Cane Corso she has ever seen in her life, rounding the kitchen corner. He was huge, male Corsos usually weighed 110 to 150lbs and this one was definitely tipping the scale at 150. She stood still not wanting the big beast to attack her and waiting for Legend to introduce the two, letting the dog get her scent. But that didn't happen, he walked out of the kitchen saying "Mo, Boss, Boss, Mo", then leaving her alone with an animal that doesn't know her and her whispering Legend's name for him to return. She stood very still as Boss walked over to her. He sniffed all around her then lay at her feet. She stood terrified not knowing what to do until he rolled over on his back with his belly up. She knew this gesture was for her to rub him. She bent down rubbing his stomach telling him how beautiful he was. After they bonded for about five minutes of her babying the massive dog she walked away going to find Legend with Boss trailing on her heels.

She found him in his bedroom located next to the room that was so called hers when she was there on the weekends, which he had beautifully decorated with her favorite colors, chocolate, mint green and beige. She didn't need to ask him why he didn't take his parents room the master bedroom of the house because she could truly understand. She didn't even attempt to walk in the direction of their bedroom. But she did grab and hug him telling him how sorry she was and how she hated that she wasn't there for him during his grieving, but even though they were apart she did grieve with him in her heart.

They finally got themselves situated in the living room on the large sectional with Mia in her normal spot, sitting right next to Legend with his arm draped around her and now with Boss lying on the floor at her feet.

"Now G, I know you don't have this big ass dog and he's soft as cotton? He gon' let anybody walk in yo' spot." she stated while rubbing her feet on the dog.

He laughed at her statement because Boss was far from a sucka. "That nigga ain't nowhere near soft, Mo. He's trained to be a killa and he was also trained to your scent and your looks. You could have stumble in here on a humble by yourself and he would not have attacked you."

She lifted herself off of him turning and asking, "How the hell did he get trained to my scent and looks?"

"From some clothing you had here and a picture of you. They went hand in hand during his training period."

"You mean to tell me he picked up my scent in clothes from years back?"

"Yes Mo, he's a dog, his sense of smell is keen and when I got him two years ago I knew I had to train him to you because I didn't want his big ass attacking you when I finally caught up to your ass. But you want to know what's crazy, Mo?"

"What?" She asked while leaning back against him.

"When I started inquiring about the female I saw Horace talking to that night and started hearing her resume of how she was the cook for niggas, how she was into the law shit and how she was taking trips for her father I should have known it was you. Once they said she was the cook baking more than ten pies at a time that should have been a red flag for me. I can remember our first cooking lesson from your dad. The shit we were taught as kids was crazy."

"Yeah, that shit was crazy but it prepared us for what our fathers must have known we were up against in these streets. And I should have known something was up six years ago when all my customers eventually started having the same quality of work when before their shit was iffy and I used to have to work miracles for them thangs to be doing something. Then once they all had the same good shit I knew every one of them was getting their shit from the same source which was the same quality we learned how to cook when we were teenagers. That should have been my red flag."

"Yeah, but you know you're going to have to stop cooking up them niggas work now."

She sat up once again looking at him with a confused look on her face, "Why would I stop doing that? That's my money G."

"I know, but think about. It was cool when you were just them niggas cook you were an asset to them they got their shit cooked up right from a pro. But now that pro is affiliated with the connect, now that makes you an asset no longer but a liability. You know how many niggas will try to hem you up trying to get at me."

She laid back down on him thinking he was absolutely right. "Well we gon' have to figure something out because I need my bread, G. And not to mention Cleveland niggas ain't the only ones I whip for. Which can be a plus for you, we can have niggas from all areas of Ohio copping from you."

"That's what's up, but don't worry about yo' bread, yo' nigga got you. We'll put something together."

Legend and Tamia stayed up most of the night catching up and filling each other in on their lives and each other's businesses. They discussed everything from her father to his disrespectful broad, to his family's storage facilities. She told him where she lived which out of coincidence was two blocks around the corner from where he lived; she also told him how she became to start fucking with the nigga Ant in Terri Haute. He told her about Quan catching a case and how he didn't want to move forward on some business ventures until he knew for sure it was just a weed case. She assured him that's all it was and how she had already did her homework on the situation. She couldn't have her best friend fucking around with a potential snitch. They also discussed his father and how something didn't sit right with him and how his mother never wanting to leave her country again, saying the United States was full of pussy men. They figured out a way for her to still play her part and continue getting her money. And they even exchanged information on their stash spots and safe combinations giving each other keys to their houses and alarm codes. They exchanged their mother's information in case either one of them had to get in contact with either woman. Nothing was off limits with these two. They vowed never to lose contact again.

When it was time for them to head to bed Mia stood to leave and go home telling Legend she would hook up with him later after she got some rest. She stood in front of him holding out her hand for a set of keys to one of his cars.

"Girl if you don't gone and go upstairs and get in yo' bed, you ain't no stranger in this house."

"I know that G, but I need to be home with my clothes."

"You got stuff in your closet and in your dresser. Anything you may need is there. Stuff like underwear, bras, shit to sleep in and shit to just throw on like jogging suits. I pick up shit here and there for my nigga keeping them updated for when we did eventually bump heads. I didn't want anything to change or be out of place, I wanted you to have stuff here like you always did. Well I hope you can fit some of the stuff because I damn sure didn't anticipate on you being so damn thick."

She gave him a, 'what the fuck look'.

"I mean you have always been a thick girl, but damn Mo."

They both laughed at the comment then headed up the stairs to call it a night.

BOSSES

Quan followed Shauntille back to her apartment asking himself over and over again what the hell took place at his party. He knew his cousin was fucking with some nigga that looked out for her but he didn't imagine that it was Legend. And now she was tripping on him talking bout he didn't do shit when Mia punched her in the face.

From his understanding the nigga she was fucking with wasn't her man, they were just cool. So if that was the case what the hell she blow up for when she saw him with somebody else. And he was only trying to calm her half crazy ass down. He thought she was doing well but the way she flipped out tonight he feel the need to call his aunt to see if her bipolar ass is still taking her medication.

He was pulled from his thoughts as he parked his car in his normal space. The moment they set foot through her front door Shauntille started with the questioning with a sad uncertain look in her eyes. "All I want to know is your cousin going to be a problem for our relationship? I mean Mia my best friend and all, but I ain't trying to lose you because she can't control that temper of hers. And it really didn't look like Legend was paying your people any attention so I hope that's not going to be a problem for y'all either."

Quan looked at her with disbelief, over the last three years he had grown to love her and considered her to be his main. But for the life of him he couldn't believe what just came out of her fucking mouth (I mean Mia my best friend and all, but...) he stopped listening to her once she said "but." To him if they were best friends it wasn't a, but. He had always been about loyalty. It was part of his upbringing so for her to incorporate but, was enough for him to take a mental note on their relationship. Yeah she was his boo and he would never let anything come between them, but for her to second guess her friendship for him, a nigga, was...., hell it really wasn't any words for it.

Now he thought of what Legend said when they were having lunch the other day. *"You better stop her from that pillow talk shit; you don't want her pillow talkin' wit' another nigga about your ass."*

TEN

Charmaine sat in the middle of her living room floor feeling defeated. She had secluded herself in her house away from the outside world not wanting to talk to anyone but her mother. She hadn't been to school nor have she been to work. She actually hasn't blessed her body with soap and water. Her body was funky, her hair was all over her head, and her eyes were swollen from all the crying she had been doing.

The only thing she has done on a consistent basis was blow up Legend's phone. All she wanted was for him to pick up and at least explain what had happened. She had been fucking with him for years and her life had been perfect. The entire time he has been in her life she hasn't had the need to take her medication. To her it was all thanks to Legend, he was her cure to having a sane life.

Now as she dialed his number for the -she don't know how many times- her mind went blank. All she wanted was him and his attention. And at that moment she figured out a way to get his focus back on her.

BOSSES

For the past two months everything had been good in Legend's world. He and Mia were inseparable, now even closer than they were as children. They slept under the same roof every night, be it his home or hers. His business had expanded ten times fold thanks to Mia. She had introduced him to some dudes she was cooking for in Toledo, Akron, Dayton, Cincinnati, Columbus, and even Bowling Green. When he inquired about how she became to do business with the out of town dudes she simply told him her father.

Top had run across different cats out of Ohio doing their Fed bid, but were still handling their business on the streets. When some mentioned how their peoples were fucking up the work on the cook side, of course he put in a good word for Mia, claiming that his daughter had the best water whip game out there. When they called she gave them their ticket price after doing a background check on them first of course.

And once she started getting that out of town play her clientele grew tremendously, now that clientele belonged to Legend. He now supplied Ohio's major cities with that grade "A" quality shit.

He drove across Superior Ave bumping Rick Ross. When the song came to the "She in love wit' a Boss so she tatted my name" Mia popped in his head. No she wasn't in love with him, in a lover's kind of way, and no his name wasn't tatted on her, but she on the other hand was for sure a boss in his book and dead smack in the middle of the sleeve going down his left arm that he had done when he was twenty, read Mo Money. Whoever observed the tatt automatically assumed it was for him to get more money, not knowing the sleeve was dedicated to his good friend and only real nigga, Tamia.

As he drove he picked up his Droid Razar phone to give her a call. He was missing her and wanted to be in her company.

Mia could hear her cell phone ringing from the bathroom but she couldn't distinguish the ring tone, so whoever it was would have to wait. There was no way she was getting out of the blazing hot bath water she was relaxing in. She and Shauntille had just worked out for a hour and a half straight at Lifetime Fitness so she really was in need of a good cleansing and some relaxation.

She slid down in the tub closing her eyes spreading her legs and welcoming the feel of her waterproof silver bullet. She held her pussy lips open with her left hand while circling the bullet around her clit with her right. The feeling the bullet gave her clit under the water was phenomenal. She moaned as the bullet sent vibrations over and around her clit. In her mind she envisioned herself playing with her pussy for the first time when she was fifteen with Legend watching in silence. That was always the vision she had during her play time. His small piercing brown bedroom eyes on her drove her insane. When she started feeling the tingling in her toes working its way up and the feel of her heart beating faster she knew she would be cumming in a matter of seconds.

Again for the second time in their lives Legend was stopped abruptly by Mia's actions. As he leaned against the bathroom doorway with his hands in his jogging pants pocket and with his right leg crossed over his left, he watched Mia pleasure herself in the bathtub.

As usual Tamia slowly opened her eyes as if it was the first time again and would envision Legend in the doorway staring at her. But this time she didn't have to. She was caught once again and just like the first time she was past the point of no return. She stared directly into Legend eyes as she moaned while her body came. And just like the first time he stared in her eyes not moving until he saw that her climax had subsided. Again he turned went to her guest bathroom jumped in the shower and jacked his dick to his nigga. But unlike the first time, they were going to see each other after.

When he got finished with his shower he threw on some basketball shorts and a wife beater then headed to find Mia.

Tamia made her way to the kitchen to make them some turkey breast sandwiches on whole wheat bread with lettuce, tomato and miracle whip. She also blended them some fruit smoothies that she now fell in love with. As she finished placing their food on the table Legend entered the kitchen. They sat down at the table in front of their food and bowed their heads as he said grace. Tamia said Amen like most Christians and Legend did the sign of The Cross, crossing from left to right, like most Roman Catholics.

After she took her first bite of her sandwich she looked up only to see he wasn't eating but staring at her.

"What's wrong G, you don't want the sandwich? Do you want me to make you something else?"

He placed her cell phone on the kitchen table directly in front of her, "Keep your phone on you at all times, Mo. I don't care if you're only going to the bathroom to take a piss, take your phone with you. ¿Entiende usted?"

"Yes I understand, G" she responded knowing that he only spoke in his Spanish language when he talked to his mother or when he was upset.

With that they both proceeded to eat their food, never mentioning what transpired in the bathroom.

BOSSES

Quan rode up Kinsman Avenue heading to Shaker Heights to go check on his cousin. His aunt had told him that she had been calling Charmaine for the past month and she wasn't answering her phone nor was she answering her door. Once he reached her home he noticed her car in her garage. Figuring she was at home, he banged and banged on her door only to get no answer like his aunt had said. He didn't want to bust down her door having the Shaker Heights police all up his ass so he decided to call Legend.

Legend felt his phone vibrating in his pocket just as him and Mia got comfortable on the couch getting ready to watch their favorite movie, Love and Basketball. He looked at the screen wondering why Quan would be calling then debating if he should answer or not.

She looked over at his screen then looked at him, "answer the call G. I know this is out of routine for him to be calling at this time, which means it could be important."

"Or suspicious," he replied.

"I told you, I did my homework. Quan is cool, please trust me." She pleaded with him.

By the time he decided to answer his phone he had already missed the call. Instead of calling back he put his phone down on the cocktail table.

Tamia looked at him sideways, she couldn't believe that he was being so stubborn about Quan catching a weed case. She had assured him a thousand times that's all it was. Shit the firm that she worked for didn't represent people who were cooperating with the police. Her firm says cooperating is only a technical word for snitching and they didn't fuck with snitches. So she knew for sure Quan was cool, not by just the homework she did, but her firm was the ones who represented him. When everything was said and done, the only thing Quan had to do was pay a punk ass weed ticket for a hundred dollars.

When his phone vibrated again, she took matters in her own hands because she knew it had to be important if Quan was calling right back.

"Hello" She said as she answered his phone.

"What's good Mia? Is yo' boy around?"

"Yeah, but he's busy. That's why I answered, so what's good?"

Quan went on to tell her about the situation with Charmaine from A to Z. He damn near told her the girls' life story about her mental disorder, her being bipolar and suicidal. And now how his aunt, his mother's only sister, is worried sick about her child because no one has seen her or talked to her in thirty days. Now all he really wants is the house key that Legend might have so he could enter her house to see if everything was okay.

She relayed the message to Legend who was still feeling suspect because he was fucking with Charmaine for seven years and not once did he notice her having a mental problem. But when he thought back to the night at his club he remembered the 360 change she had displayed, then he thought about how she called his phone for thirty days straight and then she just stopped. He hasn't gotten a call in the past thirty which was the same amount of days that her family hasn't heard from her. So he agreed to go to Charmaine's house of course with Mia coming along to give Quan the key.

Quan was relieved when he saw Legend's car pull in the driveway. He walked to the passenger side where Legend was sitting, apologizing. "Man, L, you know I wouldn't have called on any bullshit. But my aunt man, I have to honor her wishes."

"It's cool Quan. Now go make sure everything's okay." Legend said as he passed him the house key and gave him her security code.

They watched as Quan entered the house. Mia decided to wait because she didn't want anything fucked up to be going on and Quan being left there alone. And just as she thought, Quan came out of the house holding his hand on his head with tears coming down his face. They watched as he made a call on his phone and heard him telling his aunt how he found Charmaine dead in her tub with slits going up her wrist.

All Tamia could think was that Charmaine wasn't fake killing herself trying to slit across her wrist like most. Then be mad because they're in the psyche ward. She knew how to get the job done by taking the razor straight up. Mia got out of the car hugging Quan telling him how sorry she was for his lost. They stayed with him until his aunt arrived along with the paramedics and police.

Mia drove away feeling sorry for Quan. She looked over at Legend as he sat next to her in the passenger seat looking like he didn't give a fuck. At times she just didn't understand the man. A female he had been fucking for seven years had killed herself-obviously over him-but he sat there with no emotion on his face.

They reached Mia's home then picked up right where they left off. Legend put the movie back on with Mia lying against him. After all of five minutes Legend picked up his phone giving Quan a call telling him he would take care of all the funeral expenses.

She smiled on the inside, she knew her nigga wasn't that cold hearted.

ELEVEN

Legend left Mia's house around seven o'clock the next morning on his way home to relieve some stress. He had every intention to work out for about three hours. He couldn't believe or comprehend what the hell was on Charmaine's mind when she decided to take her own life. He had read the letter that she wrote and had requested that it be given to him after her death, but he was still left with no understanding. To him there was no reason. Yes he had been fucking around with her for x-amount of years, but in that same token in any of those years was she his woman? And for the most part neither was Mo she was just his nigga and if Charmaine would have just came to him in the proper fashion instead of going loco he would have introduced the two.

As he walked through the side door of his home all could be heard was Boss running down the stairs to greet him sounding like a stampede of bulls. The gigantic dog greeted his master by jumping up and resting his paws on Legend's shoulders. He shooed Boss away then escorted him out the back door so the dog could relieve his bladder. Once Boss was finished Legend through his collar and leash around his neck deciding to take him for a morning walk.

Ant sat in his Ford Taurus rental car across the street a couple of houses down from Legend's home. He watched the nigga that had been taking up to much of Mia's time.

When he arrived in Cleveland a week ago, it was to see if Mia thought anything about the proposal that he had given her two months ago. But once he arrived he could clearly see that she hasn't thought twice about what he had asked her. From what he could see in the past week of him following her around was that she already had nigga. And he must not have been taking care of her pussy very well because if he was she would not have been getting her back bent out down in The Haute by him.

By following her and this nigga around he also observed that the nigga was the fuckin' man and now he didn't give a fuck if she got at him or not. He has a new plan that he was about to put into motion.

BOSSES

Tamia was awakened by the horrible sound of her house phone ringing. She hated when people called her house phone but also knew it might be an emergency if one was calling that line. So she got out of her comfortable king size bed and proceeded to her kitchen to answer the blaring phone.

She grabbed the cordless phone from the base answering on the one hundredth ring, "Hello."

"Baby Girl, I have been calling your cell for the past thirty minutes not getting an answer, so you better start telling me something. Is everything okay wit' you?"

She smiled at the concern she heard in her daddy's voice. He knew very well if something was wrong she could take care of herself if need be. "Everything cool

Daddy, I guess I just didn't hear my cell. I was tired and was in a deep sleep. I apologize if I had you worried, but what's up? It must be kind of important if you kept calling."

"Not real important but is something that needs your attention."

"What's that?"

"Well I want to talk to you about something concerning Lil G, but I don't want to do it over the phone so I want you to come down for a visit and I also want you to do a drop while you're down here."

"I'll be there this weekend," was all she said before hanging the phone up in Top's ear.

Her father sure had her attention when he said he wanted to discuss Lil G and not over the phone. So she knew it had to be something serious. She had told her father of her hooking back up with him two months ago and how well he was doing for himself. She also mentioned how some nights Legend couldn't sleep because of thoughts of his dad's murder, because to him that's exactly what it was not a damn accident. Now she was very curious about what her father had to say to her about her nigga. After hanging up from her father she immediately picked up her cell phone to give Shauntille a call.

Shauntille was doing her usual shopping at Beachwood Mall when she heard the ring tone *Jigga, what's my muthafuckin' name* coming from her cell, knowing it was her one and only best friend. "Alright, Alright, Alright",

Shauntille answered in her usual playful tone mimicking Kevin Hart.

"What's up crazy?" Mia responded to her best friend

"Nothing much, I'm at the mall picking up a couple of items. Why, what are you up to?"

"Shit really, but I wanted to know if you were busy this weekend? I need to go see my father and wanted to know if you felt like riding shot gun?" She asked while looking at her finger nails realizing it was time for a manicure.

"I can't this weekend, kind of already have plans. But I can go next weekend if you want to postpone."

"Nawl, I need to get down there this weekend. He said he have something important to talk to me about, but I'll be cool this won't be my first solo trip."

"Are you sure? Because I can postpone my plans then if it's that important."

"Girl you cool, take care of your business and I'll see you when I get back."

"Alright, I'll call you later when I get settled in."

"That's what's up." Mia replied hanging up her phone.

BOSSES

Legend returned home with Boss from their morning walk with a thousand things on his mind. One of them was who the fuck was the nigga sitting across the street from his house trying to be incognito? He had been seeing the car around town for the past week but didn't think too much of it, but now he knew something was definitely up and he wanted to get tabs on the car and the nigga fast. He wanted to know if it was the police or some jack boy and he wanted to know ASAP.

BOSSES

Detective Reigns had been keeping tabs on the driver of the 2011 Ford Taurus ever since he saw him make a drug transaction out of the car over a week ago. By trailing the driver for the small length of time he knew this was not some small time drug dealer but also knew he wasn't the big cheese either and that's who he wanted. That would be the extra boost he needed as a new FBI agent, and now would be the perfect time for him to earn his stripes.

He heard the loud police siren over his car stereo playing then turned his attention to his rearview mirror. Once he saw the car that was pulling him over he knew it was an undercover and wanted to shit on himself.

BOSSES

Legend returned to Mia's house around midnight with his body feeling dead dog tired. The first thing he wanted to do was to hop in the shower. Once he finished his shower he proceeded to her bedroom to check on her figuring she was asleep. But unbeknownst to him she was wide awoke walking around her room packing two large duffle bags with what seemed to be prepackaged food and a lot of men items which made him know exactly what was up.

Tamia stopped in mid stride when she noticed him standing in her doorway.

"What's good G? Why you just standing there?"

He continued to stand in his location not even acknowledging her questions.

"Hello! G" She stated again, this time waving her hands in midair.

"So you're about to take a trip to Terri Haute?" He asked finally breaking his silence.

"Yeah, my Dad called and said he had some things to discuss with me and while I'm down there I'm going to do a drop for him."

As soon as she got her last words out of her mouth, he turned walking out of her bedroom and her house with an attitude.

Once she realized that Legend left the house and was not just going into another room she dialed his cell number repeatedly only for him not to answer. After dialing his number for the fifth time she gave up thinking he must have had something to do that he has forgotten about. Never giving it a second thought she flopped down on her king size bed to give her best friend a call so that they could have their usual late night girl talk.

Shauntille was sitting on her large sectional going through her DVR to see which one of her favorite TV shows she was going to catch up on first when she heard Mia's ring tone coming through her cell phone. After settling on watching *Bones* first she picked up her phone. "What's up Mia?" She asked as she pressed play on the remote.

"Nothing much, was just packing up this stuff for the weekend. Legend ass just left looking mad about something, what I don't know but I guess he just got a lot on his mind."

"Shit he's probably mad about your trip."

Looking confused Mia asked, "Why would he be mad about my trip, this ain't nothing new."

"You right but seeing as though he has a thing for you, he's probably thinking you're going to see your dick also when you get down there."

"You sound crazy Shaunie. He ain't got a thing for me, because if he had I'm pretty sure he would have said something."

"Why do you think that? You have a thing for him too and you ain't said shit." Shauntille replied as she pressed pause on the remote because she ain't paid any attention to her show.

Mia laughed at her girl because she was absolutely right. She did have a thing for Legend but she would never let him know that. "I haven't told him and I never will tell him because our friendship is way more important, but I do think I'm going to holla at him tonight because I would hate to go out of town with us on a bad note."

"Yeah I think that would be good."

"Alright Shaunie, let me finish packing this stuff and then head over to Legend's house."

The two ended their conversation with Mia handling her business and with Shauntille getting back to her recorded TV shows.

TWELVE

The weekend had come entirely too soon for Mia. She was already for her trip to Terri Haute but had some kind of reservations about not going. One was Legend. When she had went to his house the other night he wasn't there and didn't come home for the entire night. All she did while there was chill with Boss and watch television. Then on top of that she hasn't seen him for the next couple of days after which really wasn't like them. True she had spoken to him on the phone but it wasn't the same as seeing him. But it was what it was and now she needed to take that ride, so she packed up her car and jumped on the highway.

BOSSES

Quan watched Shauntille intensively as she sat on her living room floor burying her head in some paper work not paying him any attention, something that she has always done when he was in her presence. Now as he thought about it he started wondering why she was even there at all, because Legend had told him that Mia was going to see her father for the weekend. He guessed now would be the perfect time to ask why she wasn't on that ride with her best friend. "Babe, why are you here and not with Mia? Why would you let her take that long drive by herself?"

She glanced up from her stack of papers looking at Quan as if she had forgotten that he was even there. "For one Babe the drive even isn't that long and she has done it before, but a case came across my boss's desk that I felt needed my attention."

"Well I guess it's really important if your boss got you working, because I've never seen you doing work on the weekends." He stated as he stood from the couch beginning to gather his things.

"Actually my boss not even taking the case but it does have some importance to me and the firm."

With a confused look on his face he went on to inquire. "Damn, a case your boss ain't giving a fuck about got you wide open, do you care to share?"

"Not right now, but when the time is right I will and my boss do give a fuck that's why he gave it to me to handle." She replied then burying her head back into the papers so she can do some more investigating.

Quan left out of her home not even saying goodbye, and with Shauntille not even noticing.

BOSSES

Tamia dreaded the visitation process, having to wear certain clothing so that she didn't entice the prisoners, having her damn money in a dumb ass clear bag, and having to sit in a room full of people as she talked to her father. She hated seeing him under these conditions. If it was up to her she would never visit him, she would continue to play her part on the outside. But since he said it was important here she sat waiting for the guards to bring him to the visitation room.

Top finally waltzed into the room looking like he had just stepped out of a prison GQ magazine. Larry Travis is tall, dark, and handsome just as some women proclaim to like their men. That may be the very reason why he has a stable of women at his every beck and call.

As soon as she saw her father she had a smile on her face like Chester the Cat from Alice in Wonderland and once he was finally close enough she leaped into his arms. She may have hated visiting him under restricted conditions, but once she was face to face with him she was ever so grateful. She had missed him so much she had tears cascading down her face and refused to break the hold she had on him. Top rubbed his baby girl hair as she cried on his chest. He knew she had a rock solid heart, but when it came to him her heart was like a big bowl of Jell-O. Finally letting her father go she went to the restroom to clean her face. On her way back to her seat she stopped by the vending machines grabbed them some snacks then made her way to her original location. Once seated with her let's get down to business face on Mia didn't waste any time questioning her father about the information he had about Legend.

BOSSES

Shauntille couldn't believe what she was reading with her own two eyes. Out of all the people in the world she would have never thought of him being a snitch. He just seemed like a stand up kind of guy to her. A street nigga that took the good with the bad of the game and sometimes the bad was getting knocked and having to do some time. But this guy with all the heartless, fearless, bar none reputation didn't want to lay down for a punk ass two years. He'd rather turn on his peoples than to sit down for a minute on his own bullshit. As she thought about the situation she knew exactly why the nigga was snitching and the first person she was going to put on to his bullshit was Legend.

BOSSES

Tamia left the visit from her father thinking how in the hell was she going to unload some shit like that to Legend. The information was just too much. Now all she wanted to do was head back to her hotel room, sleep the night away, do the drop in the morning, then head back to Cleveland.

As she slept Ant sat outside the hotel next to her road car contemplating his next move. At that very moment all he wanted to do was go up to her room, bang on her door then ravish her body as soon as she answered. But he knew her first question would be how in the hell did he know she was in town without her phoning him. If only she knew he had a GPS attached to her car over a year ago when they were having one of their late night escapades. He wanted to know every time she entered his city. That's how he knew exactly how to find her in Cleveland. He followed the location on the GPS to her address since that's where she kept her road car parked. Once he got there and saw her parading around town with some nigga the wheels started turning in his head just as they were doing at that very moment with him sitting outside the hotel she was in.

The next morning Mia didn't even have to wait for the wakeup call. She had been up since five that morning thinking about what her father had told her, so when she did get the call she was up and out. She wanted nothing more than to get back to The Land to holla at her nigga.

BOSSES

Legend received Shauntille's message about her needing to talk to him about something important around seven o'clock that morning. After returning her call he agreed to meet her right away because of the urgency in her voice. He entered the Landmark restaurant on 55th and St. Clair forty five minutes after hanging up from her. He found her in the back of the restaurant sitting in a booth sipping on a cup of coffee. As he sat down across from her, she slid him the folder that she had her head buried in for the past couple of days. "I already ordered your food, and no I didn't order any pork."

He nodded his head the proceeded to look at the contents inside the folder. When done reading he looked up at her with a confused look on his face. What he had just read was mind boggling. *What the fuck was this nigga thinking? What the fuck part of the game was this?* He had a million and one thoughts running through his head. His mind was going a mile a minute.

She saw the confused look in his eyes and decided to be the first to speak. "I feel the same way. It's one thing for him to turn out to be a snitch, but it's another when he got a thousand people to snitch on, but he feels the need to snitch on Mia."

"Shaunie man, I don't know what this is about, but you know I ain't baring none of it. I don't tolerate that tattle telling shit anyway, but for this muthafucka to think he's about to tell on my nigga is fuckin' loco. The nigga don't know it but he just signed his own death warrant."

Legend left Shauntille sitting in the restaurant not even caring about some damn food. Breakfast was the furthest thing from his mind at this point.

BOSSES

Tamia pulled off the highway. For some reason her stomach was feeling awkward. True she hadn't ate anything as of yet, just drunk some bottled water that she already had in the car from the night before. But she felt that wasn't a reason for her stomach to be feeling fucked up and on top of that she was also feeling dizzy. After putting her car in park once she reached the gas station she decided that she must need to put something on her stomach before she head back on the road. She unlocked her car doors to get out but for some reason she couldn't move. She tried and tried again but her body wouldn't do what her brain was telling it to. She felt someone open her door and to her surprise it was Ant. She gave him a slight smile and tried to open her mouth to speak but wouldn't shit come out.

Ant reached inside the car to help her out asking her what she was doing in his neck of woods and didn't get at him. She tried to answer him but of course wouldn't anything leave her lips. And then all type of alarms went off in her head. It didn't take a rocket science to figure out that she had been drugged. She watched in her sedated state as he guided her to his truck as one of his boys jumped in her car. All she could think was *damn this nigga was serious when he said he wanted me down here with him but is it really this fuckin' serious.* He smiled at her after strapping her in the backseat of his truck. He jumped in the driving seat then sped off.

BOSSES

As Legend pulled in his driveway he knew what exactly had to be done and it had to be done fast. He didn't even want Mia to catch wind of the shit. He was going to handle this shit ASAP. So he picked up his phone to make a call.

"Hello."

"Did you make it back to the house yet?" He asked as he stroked his beard.

"No, but I'm in route. What's up?"

"Well swing my way, I'll let you in on what I want when you get here."

THIRTEEN

Tamia blacked out no less than ten minutes of being in Ant's truck. How long she was out she had no idea but when she woke up she was lying on a dirty, musty, smelly full size mattress inside of a small dark room. This time when she tried to move her limbs they were working so, she sat up on the mattress to survey her surroundings. She checked her body noticing all of her clothing was still covering her body. Where she was she had no idea but what she wanted was answers and she wanted them fast. She stood walked over to the door and banged on it as hard as she could.

BOSSES

Shauntille looked at her caller ID on her cell phone wondering who the fuck was calling her. She had never seen the number a day in her life. Not knowing who the caller was she sent the call straight to her voicemail. Maybe they would leave a message or maybe they won't, either way she wasn't trying to hear from whoever it was because she had a call to make her own self. She had been dialing Tamia's number for the past 24 hours straight and knows she should have been back from her trip. Figuring that something could have went wrong while doing a drop she finally decided to try Top's number, praying that everything was good.

"What's up Shaunie girl? What did I do to deserve this call?"

"Hey Dad, I was trying to see was everything cool down there, because I haven't talked to Mia yet and I have been calling her cell all night and day. She should have been back in town from seeing you by now."

"Everything down here went smooth Shaunie. But she did tell me that she was stopping to see one of her male friends when she made it back to town. She said she was going to sit with him for a while and cook him some dinner, said the nigga had been complaining about how she wasn't spending enough time with him. But Shauntille soon as you talk to her tell her to call me right away. I don't like that shit, I don't care what nigga she laid up with she is to always answer her damn phone. You hear me Shaunie? I mean as soon as you talk to her."

"I hear you Dad."

Shauntille hung up the phone with Top knowing that Mia wasn't cooking any nigga dinner but was cooking up some dope. But something was still wrong with that situation because she would always let Shauntille know when she was somewhere handling business. Just in case of an emergency.

Exiting highway 480 west heading towards his spot in Olmstead Falls Horace felt his cell vibrating on his waist. He looked at the screen turning up his face. He knew the number, but wanted to know why they would be calling him. And he also wondered how they knew his number, he knew how he got a hold of theirs but there wasn't any reason for them to have his. He decided to answer the call thinking that something had to be definitely wrong for them to be calling him.

"Hello" He answered as he took a pull from his tightly rolled loud stick.

"May I speak to Horace?" Shauntille asked knowing it was him answering the phone

"This him. Who this?"

"What's up Horace? This Shauntille, I don't mean to bother you or anything, but I wanted to know if you heard from Mia? She hasn't been answering her phone." She asked looking annoyed by the sound of his voice.

Looking at his cell puzzled Horace asked, "Why would you be calling me if she's not answering her phone? Maybe she's taking care of some business or getting fucked. Hell I don't know."

Now she was really annoyed, she hated his smart ass mouth. He should have known if she was calling him it must be of some type of importance. Why else would she be calling his corny ass? Yeah he a nigga that's about a dollar and his street credibility reach is long, but she could see all through his bitch ass. Hating ass, soft ass nigga, she knew he had a thing for Mia but his bitch ass too scary to say anything to her. He'd rather stalk from a distance and then pull a bitch ass move when he sees something he doesn't like, corny ass nigga.

"Well I know for sure she's not getting fucked and I kind of figured she is handling business. That's why I'm calling you because I know your spot is probably the only spot she feels comfortable in to not feel the need to let anyone know where she is and not answer her phone."

He smiled at the thought. He liked hearing that she was only comfortable at his spot.

He arrived at his destination and hopped out of his car smiling from ear to ear as he talked to Shauntille on the phone.

"I guess you're right, and she is supposed to come by my spot after she gets back in town from seeing her dad. I left everything she needed but I didn't think she was going to go straight there from the highway. But I guess she wanted to get it over with. You know your girl's motto, make money now and rest later. I'll go out there after I change my clothes and tell her you're looking for her. Is that cool?"

"Yeah that's cool. Tell her to call me ASAP. And thanks Horace, I really do appreciate this." Shauntille replied waiting for a response hating the fact that she had to be on the phone with his sorry ass.

BOSSES

"Well, well, look who's finally up and about." Ant spoke as he approached the door that Tamia was banging on. "I'm telling you now Mia act like you got some damn sense when I open this door. I'm not trying to hurt you. I have some things to discuss with you that are short and simple. Now I'm about to open the door and please remember I'm not trying to hurt you, but Mia I promise I'll shoot you dead between the eyes if you don't cooperate."

Tamia moved away from the door, went back to sit on the dirty mattress with her back against the wall, folding her legs Indian style and sat in silence.

He listened to her movements on the other side of the door sensing that she sat back down, and took her lack of response as she understood every word that came out of his mouth. He opened the door slowly then walked inside the small room.

She looked at him with a blank face, "So what things do you have to discuss with me?"

"I want to discuss your boyfriend." Ant said as he sat down in a chair in the corner of the room.

She looked at him with a confused with a 'what the fuck are you talking about' look on her face. "First of all I don't have a boyfriend seeing as though I'm not a child, but you're going to have to give me more than that if you want to discuss something."

"I don't think now is the time for your smart ass sarcastic mouth. I want to know about that gettin' money nigga I saw you riding around Cleveland with." He replied as he pulled out his chrome 380 with an extended clip resting it on his thigh.

The sight of the pistol didn't scare her one bit. She actually looked at the gun and smiled.

"Well since you were in my territory following me around and now have me locked up in this musty ass room, I take it you know everything you need to know about him. So now all you have to do is, pick up my phone, go through the recent calls, find the name Legend, press the call button, and tell the man what is that you want."

He stood from the chair, headed towards the door, then looked back at her, "You're absolutely right." He walked out of the room doing just as she suggested.

Tamia pulled her knees to her chest and shook her head thinking, *Dumb muthafucka.*

BOSSES

Legend stood in the corner of the parking garage waiting patiently for his prey to arrive. He adjusted the black skully on his head to make sure it was secure and he made sure that the face mask covering his nose and lips was also secure. He then pulled the hoodie a little lower over his face so that all that could be seen was his dark piercing eyes. He gripped his 9mm tightly in his right hand and stood very still against the brick wall of the garage waiting for the perfect moment to put a bullet straight threw his intended victims head.

He stalked his victim as they pulled their 2011 Ford Taurus in its assigned parking space then exited the car.

He walked behind his victim not making any type of sound. The dumb muthafucka talked to someone on their cell phone not focused and not realizing that they were being followed.

As he got closer he figured he really didn't want to shoot his gun because he had another plan in mind. So he tucked his pistol in the waist band of his jeans and pulled out his Benchmade 51 Morpho Balisong Butterfly knife. He got as close as he could and grabbed his victims head then slashed their throat. He slid them to the ground and then proceeded to pull out their tongue through the open wound of their throat, giving them a famous Colombian necktie.

He stepped on the victims phone crushing it then stepped over them leaving them lying on the garage floor dead. He left the parking garage just as quiet as he came. He made it to his smug that he had parked around the corner. As he started the car and drove off he shook his head.

Shauntille laid her phone on her kitchen counter the moment she heard his hit the ground, knowing that Horace life was no more. She jumped off the bar stool heading to her bedroom to grab her carrying on bag and the big vanilla folder that lay across her bed.

He didn't want to kill. He hated having to get physical. He just wished everybody played by the same set of rules, especially his. If they did then everything would run smoothly. But seeing as though they didn't, muthafuckas had to go. Snitching was never an option in the game he was playing and since muthafuckas couldn't control their tattle telling ass tongues he gave them a little assistance. But Horace, out of all people should have known better. He should have known his life was over the very moment he formed an alliance with the FBI and put Mia's name in his mouth on some ill shit at that.

And if the dumb bastard didn't know anything at all he should have known he was fucking with a Boss, because Legend was far from anything else.

As he hopped on 480 East, he shook his head some more not understanding Horace's actions. He figured he'd give Mia a call to let her know he would be stopping by her house later. He has gone long enough not being in his nigga's company. When he picked up his phone to dial her number he noticed she was already calling him. He had totally forgotten about silencing his phone earlier that day.

"What's up Mo? I was just about to call you."

"This ain't Mo my dude, but I am someone you need to be gettin' at."

Legend sat on the phone listening to the nigga's list of demands. He hung up the phone then banged his hand on his steering wheel. He looked at his reflection in his rearview mirror shaking his head once again.

"What the fuck is wrong wit' muthafuckas? What the fuck is the world coming to? What is it, fuck with Legend day? These niggas must think I'm soft of something. Guess I have myself another nigga I have to kill. After this Mia is sitting her ass down. She's going take her ass to school full time, get her degree, and keep her ass out of the damn streets. That's my final word." He spoke out loud to himself.

He then placed an important call to some important people. This Terri Haute nigga had him fucked up, kidnapping Mo, really? Now he was about to feel the wrath of the Dominican Cartel.

FOURTEEN

Quan decided to place a call to Shauntille. He was missing his lil boo. They really haven't been spending anytime together and when he did stop buy her spot she seemed to be preoccupied and too busy to him pay any attention.

Shauntille heard her cell singing Mr. Wrong. Knowing it was Quan she pressed the ignore button sending him straight to her voicemail. She didn't have time to talk to him at the present moment. She was trying to hurry out the door so she wouldn't miss her flight.

Once she got in her car her cell started again. She looked at the caller ID noticing it was Legend so she decided to answer.

"Shauntille, where you at? I need to talk to you right now it's very important."

"Well I can't stop and talk right now L, I'm on my way to the airport and I can't afford to miss my flight."

"Man, fuck yo' flight. I said I need to talk to you now. Meet me at Mo's. Like right now!" He yelled at her as he hung up his phone not waiting for a response.

She threw her cell in the passenger seat mad as hell and headed straight to Tamia's house. Just like Legend instructed.

Ant opened the door to where he was keeping Tamia. He looked at her only to see she was sitting in the same position she was in when he left. He sat in the chair across from her and stared at her. As he looked at her he realized how much he loved her. He had every intention of going to Cleveland and expressing to her how he felt about her. Yeah what they had was just a fuck thing, but he knew it could have been so much more. He had money and lots of it, he had bitches and lots of those too, he had baby mommas five to be exact, but the one thing he didn't have was the female who has been giving him the best pussy he has ever had for the past couple of years. And that's exactly what he wanted, for her to be his woman. But no, this whore already had a dude. Not to mention a rich one at that. When he told the nigga he wanted a million for Mia and the nigga agreed he knew he hit the jack pot. But what he didn't understand was if she had a nigga like that in her corner why the fuck was she fucking him?

"Let me ask you something?" He stated with his elbows resting on his knees looking dead in her face.

She looked up at him with a slight smile on her face, "What's that?"

"Why were you down here fucking me if you had a dude? A dude that's about drop a mill for your whorish ass I might add."

She kept with her facial expression answering, "You know what I can't even answer that for you, I don't have any idea why I was down here fucking yo' soon to be dead ass."

"If I was you I would watch my mouth, yo' ass go' be here for another two days, and if you keep up wit' that smart shit I can make those days very unbearable for you. Do you understand?"

Tilting her head to the side she asked "That's the deadline you gave him?"

"Yeah, so if I was you, I'll keep that smart shit to a minimum." He replied as he stood up from the chair getting ready to leave the room.

"I got you. I'll keep my words to a minimum." She responded as she leaned her head back down knowing she wasn't going to be there for no two days and also knowing this stupid muthafucka would be dead within the next five hours.

BOSSES

Legend sat inside of Tamia's house patiently with two of his uncles waiting for Shauntille to show up.

She walked inside of Mia's house upset. She really needed to get down to Terri Haute.

"What's up L, I really need to be getting out of here."

"Where you such in a rush to get to Shaunie damn, I'm trying to get some info out of you so I can go get Mo." He stated annoyed by her actions.

"Wait, what do you mean so you can go get Mo, you know where she's at?" She asked with a questioning look on her face.

"Yeah the nigga she was fucking with in Terri Haute called me from her phone demanding a ransom."

"I knew it." She replied then ran out of the door.

He looked at his uncles like what the fuck. He began to go after her but just as fast as she ran out the door she was running back in.

Out of breathe she started talking a mile a minute as she began to unload some the contents she had in the folder.

"See L that's where I was on my way to. I was going to do some scoping out, and then I was going to call you down there. I wanted to make sure my gut feeling was right before I involved you."

Legend held his hand up, "Wait Shaunie slow down, you was on your way where?"

"Down to Terri Haute, I knew something was up when Mia didn't return so I called her dad thinking maybe the drop went bad and she got arrested. But when Top told me everything went cool with the drop, but Mia did tell him that she had to do some cooking when she got back. He thought maybe that's where she was taking care of some business. But I knew that couldn't have been the case seeing as though she would have never in a million years went to take of business and not let me know where she was. And she would have never in a millions years not have called me at all in this length of time, not to mention not answering her phone when I called. So I was going down there to do a little snooping to see where Ant head was. When we were there two months ago Mia mentioned to me that he was giving her sixty days about their thing.

But she wasn't paying him any attention, she wasn't on him like that. But I could have sworn I saw him in our city about two weeks ago. I let it go thinking nawl that wasn't him, because he has never came up here. But with her going down there and not returning I figured something had to be up. And the more I think about it that was his ass I saw driving, a silver Taurus with out of town plates on it." Shauntille blurted out it seemed like all in one breath.

"You said a silver Taurus?" Legend asked as he stroked his beard. "You might be absolutely right because I saw a nigga in a silver Taurus sitting outside of my house trying to be incognito."

"Yeah that had to be his ass and this is everything I have on him." She said as she spread all the contents of the folder out on the counter.

He looked at everything she had. This girl had everything on his parents who were still living and married and also living in the same household to which she had the address to. She had the addresses to not one but all of his baby momma's spots. She had the whereabouts to all three of his siblings. She even had information on niggas that he ran with, how many cases they all done caught and all of their addresses and baby momma addresses. This girl wasn't playing.

He looked at her, "Shauntille, I motherfucking love you. You just don't know. This is all the ammunition I need. That nigga, his entire family, his niggas, their entire families, will all be dead less than three hours." He then smiled and gave her a hug, "Quan talking about you a square, shit you a little undercover Boss yourself, uh Ms. Shaunie?"

Shauntille laughed at his statement, "Not undercover just sophisticated and I like him thinking I'm a square so let's keep it that way."

With that being said Legend and his uncles left to bring his nigga back home.

BOSSES

Legend exited his family's private plane in Terri Haute two hours after leaving Tamia's house. He jumped in a car that one of his cousins had waiting for him. He placed a few calls while his cousin drove to make sure everyone was in place. He wanted this plan to be executed fast and simple because this nigga Ant had him fucked up. Yeah he could have easily paid the nigga the money for Mo's return but no he wasn't going to that. It was now time for him to make an example. You don't fuck with his family and Mo was definitely part of his family. Now this nigga and his niggas families will be all dead, babies and all. All because one muthafucka caught feelings and wanted to be greedy.

Mia could hear Legend's ringtone faintly coming from her phone. She heard Ant answer the phone with much aggression in his voice. She then heard him unlocking the door to the room she was secluded in. But once he entered the room she didn't see any signs of aggression on his face. He actually looked scared shitless. She stood up from the dirty mattress then held out her hand for the phone. As he handed her the phone in slow motion, she could see all the wheels spinning in his head. She then snatched the phone out of his hand.

"Dumb muthafucka."

"What's good Mo? You cool?" Legend asked with his raspy voice on the other end of the phone.

"Yeah I'm good," she answered as she looked at her watch, "You're two hours early. I underestimated you."

"Now why would you do something like that, especially with you involved?"

"I don't even know G, and since that's the case I know you brought me a present, right?"

"I sure did so come open up the door."

She left out of the small room with Ant still standing there looking shocked to go open the front door for Legend.

The moment she opened the door she smiled then held out her hand for her present. He gave her what she wanted then followed her back to the small room.

Ant sat in the chair with his head in his hands. He couldn't understand how in the hell did they know where his parents stayed. Once he heard his mother's screams through the phone he knew what had to be done. Fuck that million and let Tamia go.

He looked up from the chair wondering why Mia and her dude were walking back into the room. The agreement was for him to give her the phone and let her walk out on her own free will. After that they would let his parents go. But what he didn't know was that The

Dominican Cartel wasn't just at his parent's house but was placed at his baby mommas houses, his siblings houses, his niggas houses, and their family houses as well, all waiting for the okay from Legend.

Mia walked and stood behind Ant.

"My dude, what now, I let her go, now what do you want?" He asked looking up at Legend.

Legend shrugged his shoulders, "I don't want nothing, but she does."

Before he could even turn his head in Mia's direction she grabbed his head slitting his throat from ear to ear with her Benchmade 32 Mini-Mopho Bali-Song Butterfly knife.

She and Legend walked out of the small brick house side by side as if it was theirs. Legend nodded his head to one of his cousins standing across the street leaning against a tree giving him the okay.

FIFTEEN

Quan knocked on Shauntille's door ready to get some answers. Her not paying him any attention was not part of the deal. He knows he was the one on some bullshit at first, questioning her loyalty. But he got over it. Now she was the one on some bull, what her reasons are he don't know but he sure was ready to find out.

She had just gotten out of the shower when she heard someone banging on her door so she threw her robe on and went to answer the door. She knew it wasn't anyone but Quan so she opened the door only to see him standing there with an angry look on his face. He brushed pass her bumping her shoulder then situated his self on her couch.

"Well okay then," Shauntille said as she closed the door. She stood at the door for a while looking at Quan wondering what his issue was. As she stood there she remembered the last couple of times he was over she was busy not giving him any attention, so she walked over to the couch and straddled his lap. She rubbed her fingers over his neat dreads then slowly moved her hands down cupping his face. She tilted his head back giving him soft kisses on his lips.

She really did love Quan and knew he was the one for her and she didn't want anyone else.

She nibbled her way to his ear, "Babe I'm sorry if I haven't been giving you all the attention you deserve, but some important things with Mia came up. Baby I had to look out for my girl before I could even concentrate on anything else." She worked her way back to his lips, "You could understand that can't you? She's my best friend so I had to play my part. Please tell me you understand?" She asked now looking him directly in the eyes.

He didn't have the slightest idea about what was going on or what she was talking about, but her showing her loyalty to her best friend was enough not to be mad anymore.

He slid his hands between them unbuckling his pants and pulling out his dick, he then guided his lil boo down his tool. He knew there wasn't any need for foreplay to get her wet because her pussy stayed dripping.

She threw her head back the moment he slid inside of her. She loved the feel of his thick dick. She guided herself up and down his dick real slow.

"Yes Quan...I apologize baby...ooh I missed this dick so much...please tell me you understand...ooh yes...right there."

He had her ass cheeks gripped so tight and wasn't going to let go anytime soon. He always loved the way she rode his dick, she had the tightest wettest pussy he has ever had. That was one of the very reasons he refused to ever leave her alone. He didn't want anybody getting any of his pussy.

"Damn baby...ride that dick...damn Shaunie you about to make me bust already...damn I missed this pussy baby."

She knew it had been awhile since they last had sex and she knew he wasn't going to be able to hold back. That was always good with her because she also knew for the second round he was going to be digging her out for about an hour.

"Cum for me then baby...but please tell me, you understand." She started grinding on him faster begging for his nut with her pussy.

"Fuck me baby...damn...just like that...ooh just like that."

"Tell me you understand...I have to know...yes baby...because when something...ooh yes...come up...you have to know I will always ride with my girl." Shauntille bounced on his dick bringing her pussy to the tip real slow then slamming her pussy down real fast. "Tell me you understand," she demanded.

"Yes...yes...yes...I understand baby...damn." Quan hollered as he bust his first nut for the night.

Shauntille smiled knowing she had just worked his dick. Now she was ready to go the bedroom and prepare for round two.

BOSSES

The first thing Tamia did when she got home was jump in the shower. She felt dirty all the way around. Even dirty from the conversation she had to have with Legend on their flight home about his father. She felt even dirtier having to tell him about his father after all the other shit he had just been through. He told her about the bullshit Horace was pulling and how he took care of that, only to have to go through the Ant bull right after. And what did she do after all that, tell him the ill news she learned from her father. She stood in the shower hating herself for what she had placed on his heart.

After finishing her shower she stepped in her bedroom only to find Legend sitting on her bed writing. He looked as if he was in deep thought. She didn't want to disturb him so she gathered her things so she could get dressed in the guest room.

As she walked past the television the CNN news caught her attention. They were reporting the disturbing news of fifty houses with families still inside going up in flames at the very same time in Terri Haute, Indiana. She gave a slight smile at what she was hearing then proceeded to head to the guest room.

"Where you going Mo?" Legend asked looking up from the notebook he was writing in.

"In the other room to get dressed, I didn't want to disturb you."

"You didn't want to disturb me uh." He repeated her words as he stood leaving the notebook on her bed. "Yeah I here you Mo, but you don't have to leave out of your room. I was about to head out anyway I need to pack for our trip and so do you. We're leaving first thing in the morning."

"We're leaving in the morning, where are we going?" She asked with a confused look on her face.

"To the Dominican Republic, I need some answers from my mother," was the last thing he said before leaving out of her room with her standing there looking confused.

She finally started to move her feet once she digested what he had said. She walked over to her bed putting her things down. "I guess I better start packing then."

After putting her pajamas on she noticed the notebook that Legend had left on the bed. Sitting on the bed she picked it up and began to read.

Mo,

Can I

Touch you

Feel your feelings

Touch your inner being; being all I can be for you and all you would want me to be for you

Can I

Be the one who makes you drip from the very thought of me, of us

Can I

Kiss you in those hidden places that's buried deep within your heart

Can I

Please touch you if not physically then mentally bringing forth the thought of the possibility, the chance of me touching you

Can I?

Tamia couldn't believe what she just read. And with all the love that she has for him, he should have known that he didn't even have to ask. So hell yeah he could and the perfect place to show him will be while they were in the Dominican Republic.

A DIVINE PRODUCTION PRESENTS

DOMINICAN CARTEL

THE SEQUEL TO LEGEND

SHENETTA MARIE

In The Lab

A DIVINE PRODUCTION PRESENTS

Her

PROMISE

SOME PROMISES ARE MEANT TO BE BROKEN
VOL. 1

A NOVEL BY

SHENETTA MARIE

Available Now

ONE

Divine sat in the VIP area of the Mirage on the Water down on the West Bank of the Flats supposedly celebrating her 21st birthday but she really wasn't in the festive mood. Everyone was there enjoying her party except for her and she really couldn't understand why. Just a week ago she was surprised with a new toy, a 2011 Black on Black 745 BMW. She had more clothes, shoes, purses and accessories than a department store itself, but still she was sitting at her own party looking like she had lost her best friend. Thinking to herself *this is some bullshit, why the fuck am I sitting here not enjoying myself at my own damn party*. Divine stood walked over to the bar ordered herself a double shot of Remy Martin VSOP, threw it back and headed for the dance floor. On her way she noticed everyone poppin' champagne or throwing back shots. She received some wuz ups, head nods, peace signs and Happy Birthdays, but she wasn't stopping to politic with anyone. She was about to enjoy the rest of her night out on the dance floor.

As soon as her feet touched the dance floor, the DJ gave shout outs to all the Gemini in the building and then started with his Reggae selections as if he had read her mind and knew that Reggae was her favorite music to dance to. Instantly she started winding and twisting her waist dipping down low and winding up slow with her eyes closed imagining she was at home dancing alone. This was her first time dancing in public because whenever she went out she kind of always stayed to herself observing her surroundings. Soon as she started dancing all eyes were on her. Her dance was so exotic and seductive that no one in the club could take their eyes off her. She even had the females' attention. She was what some called every man's dream and every woman's nightmare.

Divine stood at 5'7" 175lbs, small in the waist and very, very, thick in the hips. Not only did she have the body she was also beautiful in the face. Pecan brown skin, small almond shaped eyes, the perfect size nose not too big or not too small, thin lips, and a beautiful strong jaw structure with high cheek bones. She kept her hair rinsed jet black and cut in an edgy cropped cut to show off her facial features. She was what men in the 70's called a brick house. Tonight this brick house sported a black BCBG Max Azria mid-thigh silk-nylon dress, with Gucci leather booties, simple pair of one karat diamond stud earrings and a right arm full of thick and thin gold bangles all making her look like an Amazon Goddess.

Promise looked over his right shoulder to see what all the commotion was that had everybody's attention. Once he saw what everyone was looking at he hopped off his bar stool and headed straight to the dance floor.

Divine felt a strong hand on her wrist and knew exactly who it belonged to. When she opened her eyes and saw the evil upset look staring back at her she started to panic, "Don, what's wrong, what happened?"

Never responding to her line of questioning he led her off the dance floor straight to the VIP area gathered her things then walked her out of the club to his truck only saying, "Go home".

"Go home! What the hell you mean go home? Don, what the fuck is going on?"

"I'm not going to repeat myself." Was his only reply before slamming the truck door in her face mad as shit.

He walked back inside the club not knowing if he was coming or going. Once he got back to his bar stool he ordered himself three shots of Remy downing them one after the other. *What the hell was Baby Doll thinking? Shakin' her ass like that in front of all these motherfuckers* was all he was thinking to himself.

❧❧❧❧❧❧

At home pacing the living room floor, Divine dialed Promise's number repeatedly why she didn't know because all she kept receiving was his voice mail. "Okay let me call Sin then," she said out loud.

"Wuz up wit' you Twin? Why you dip from our party so early?" Sincere asked as he took another shot of Grey Goose to the head.

"I ain't dip shit. Promise crazy ass put me out. What the hell is up with your boy?"

"I can't even answer that for you Doll. All I know is I saw the nigga throwing back shots like they wasn't shit and you and I both know that the nigga can't hold liquor worth shit. I stepped to him asking him what wuz up but he said everything was cool. Then I asked about you and he said you was tired and went to the house.

"What! Alright Twin I'll get up with you tomorrow."

"Yup"

TWO

Everyone sat in their regular seats in attendance at the big house ready to get down to business. Well everyone expect for Divine. Her not being there had everybody with a questioning look on their faces.

After being about 15 minutes late someone finally spoke about her whereabouts.

"Man this isn't like Baby Doll to be late. Hell she is the one that's always here early talking about our asses being late. I'm about to give her a call," Sincere said as he picked up his phone dialing her number.

"What's up Sin? I was just about to give y'all a call."

"Why, you on your way or something?"

"Nawl, I'm going to sit this one out. We can hook up later and you can give me the updates then," she explained while looking over the breakfast menu in front of her.

With concern in his voice, "So why you not coming through, everything cool, right?"

"Yeah everything cool, stomach just messed up from last night. So I'm in the Muslim's Spot getting ready to eat me some food."

"You know we ordered food, so why the hell you just didn't eat here?"

"Cause I didn't want to sit around y'all all sick trying to discuss business and not being able to concentrate. I was just going to grab me something real quick and head back to the house, but I ran into one of my peps from Quincy so I'm going to eat here and kick it with him for a sec."

"Cool, just call me later when you're feeling better and I'll stop by your spot to fill you in."

"Alright, I talk to you later."

As soon as Sincere closed his phone Promise was on him. "Where she at, is she on her way?"

"Nope, said her stomach is fucked up from last night and she doesn't want to sit around us sick not being able to focus so she's sitting this one out. Said she's out having breakfast with a friend."

"What the hell you mean having breakfast with a friend?" Promise asked with his face screwed up.

"Shit nigga I don't know, I wasn't questioning her all like that. My main concern was to make sure she was cool. And come to think about it, why you didn't know she was fucked up and wasn't coming? Y'all do live in the same damn house."

Promise sat through the entire meeting with his mind somewhere else mad as hell. *Who was Baby Doll out with and not handling her fuckin' business?*

The meeting was adjourned with everyone leaving except for Promise. He really couldn't even tell what the hell went on in the meeting because his mind was on Divine. The main question rolling around in his head was who and what is so God-damn important that she was missing a meeting because he wasn't buying that sick shit. Then asking himself why is the (Who?) part of the question so important to him. Well he knew why. He didn't trust niggas around his Baby Doll even though he knew she could take care of herself. She was one of them. She treated niggas like they treated hoes but he still didn't like the idea of one of them finally making their way into her heart. Because even though she didn't know it now her heart belonged to him.

He thought back to the beginning. Remembering his first time ever seeing Divine. Her aunt and cousins had moved in next door to his family on 140th and Kinsman on his 10th birthday. And once he saw her he said Happy Birthday to himself. They introduced themselves to each other, her family and his. He stared at her saying she looked like a baby doll so that's what he began to call her and soon so did everyone else. The only problem was she was two years older than him and she had quickly adopted him as her play little brother, that and the fact that she only came over on the weekends because she actually lived on Quincy with her mother and grandmother.

Their families became close real quickly his mother and her aunt, his sisters and her female cousins, his brothers and her male cousins, and Divine with all the Green Boyz. She was different from all the other girls. She was a straight tomboy wanting to do anything and everything the Green Boyz was doing. Nobody could catch her with a damn doll or playing house with the girls. She was with the boys jumping off garages on mattresses, throwing rocks at cars, building club houses, going bike riding in different hoods, and when they had become of age she was out trapping getting money with them. The Green Boyz always protected her and would kill something if any harm came her way. Especially Promise Dontae

Green and Sincere Mitchell-Green. She was so tight with the Green family some would have thought she had their blood running through her veins and when her aunt moved away to another house she still made her way back to Kinsman County to kick it with the Green Family.

When she turned eighteen she and Promise had gotten a two bedroom condo in Beachwood together. He didn't see any reason for her to move in by herself paying all that rent and he was only sixteen so he needed her name on the lease anyway. He actually preferred her name on the lease. He might have only been sixteen but he had damn near been on his own since he was thirteen. He could have had any one of his clucks to put the condo in one of their names, but he wanted it in Divine's.

He smiled to himself thinking about the past but that smile easily faded now thinking about the present. Divine had missed a family meeting to be around a nothing ass nigga doing some nothing ass shit which was unacceptable in his eyes.

THREE

Divine sat at her kitchen island enjoying a vegetable omelet with cheese wondering how in the hell a week had gone past since the last time she had talked to or even seen Promise. She knew that she had been a little busy kickin' it with her nigga Black from Quincy for the past week but it wasn't that serious that the two wouldn't have bumped heads. They did live together which made her know that he was avoiding her and now it was time for her to find out why.

Once she was done with her breakfast she had to run straight to the toilet and throw up. *Damn I haven't had shit to drink in a week so why is my stomach still fucked up.* After throwing up she took a nice hot shower then she got dressed for the day. She really wasn't doing shit that day so she decided to throw on a pair of Bold Curve Levi Slim jeans, a wife beater tank top, and a pair of Une Plum wedges by Christian Louboutin. In her ears were her signature one carat diamond studs. She un-wrapped her hair and played with her crop style cut, grabbed her red envelope purse, and threw on some clear MAC lip gloss. Simple was always her motto. If a female went all out the way with all that make up shit and too many accessories she was trying too hard and in her eyes why make it hard when it's easy. With that she was on her way out the door to see what the hell was up with her Promise.

Leaving her condo she decided to take the long way back to the hood. Instead of driving straight down Chagrin she made a right on Richmond Rd to South Woodland. She loved riding down that street. South Woodland had the most beautiful homes with beautiful manicured lawns. Those were the home where legal money and stable families lived and that's where she wanted to be in a couple of years. Yeah she enjoyed the street life and the fast money but at the end of the night she always fantasized about having children and owning her own business doing the true American family life thing and not the street family life. Even though she wouldn't change her street Fam for nothing in the world. She hoped one day they could all sit back and be normal, whatever that was anyway because her life was never truly normal. She just hoped that one day it would be. Thinking about being normal made her snap back to reality, because that day sure wasn't going to be one, fucking around with Promise crazy ass.

She couldn't even think of any possible reason why he was avoiding her besides that bullshit he pulled at her birthday party. But she was over it and it wasn't even that serious that he couldn't show his face at the place he lays his head at night. It wasn't like him to hold a grudge, well at least not one with her anyway. She could admit though that for the past couple of months he had been acting a little weird. He had always been overprotective of her. All the Green Boyz were for that matter but lately Promise had been a little extreme with his shit.

Riding down 146th street Promise was damn near run off the road at the stop sign on the corner of Milverton by this crazy ass broad driving a Dodge Stratus GT running her mouth on her cell phone. He decided he would play for a little while to kill some time and to get his mind off Divine.

He jumped out of his truck and walked up to the female's car, "Hey Sweetheart, you need to get off that phone running yo' mouth and apologize to me for running me off the road."

"Hold on girl let me check this dude real quick because I don't know who he thinks he's talking to." The yapping female said into her phone. When she went to so call check the guy the cat quickly caught her tongue. She couldn't believe her eyes *this nigga is fine as hell* she thought to herself.

"Excuse me, but are you talking to me?"

"Yes, I'm talking to you Sweetheart," He replied while standing in his cocky b-boy stance. He wore an all-black V-neck Gucci t-shirt, some hard cut Levi's, an all-black New York Yankees pro model cap and some black Gucci boots. No matter what time of year it was he always kept boots on his feet. He never knew when he had to stomp a nigga out. "So what's up Sweets, are you going to get out and say you sorry or are you going to keep running yo' mouth to that nobody on the phone?"

"Let me call you back", the female said into the phone. As she parked her car she thought to herself *damn this nigga sexy ass fuck and I don't even like yellow ass niggas.*

As soon as ole girl was out of the car she started apologizing "I'm so sorry, I really wasn't paying attention."

"It's cool Sweetheart as long as I can get a name to match that sexy face." *Sweetheart you ain't sexy at all just an average looking broad.* He couldn't keep his smile off his face. See he was a very observant man. He had seen ole girl speeding up and down Kinsman's 40's streets lately so he figured she was new to the area and he needed another trap spot.

"Well yes you can get a name. It's Carmen."

"Carmen huh, that's cool."

"Thanks and what's yours?"

"Donnie. So where yo' man at Sweetheart?"

"He's probably with his other girlfriend. And you where your woman at Boo?"

Looking at his watch he replied, "My Queen is taking care of business right now."

"Your Queen," she replied with a confused look on her face. She wasn't used to men referring to their women in that term.

"Yes, my Queen. Why is that a problem for you?"

"Nope, your Queen as you call her is your problem not mines. I told you I had a dude anyway."

"Well since that's settled we might as well exchange numbers and go on about our day because for real Sweets I need to get back to business."

Carmen left feeling like she was in love already. There was something about that nigga that made her want to call her dude and tell him to go and kill himself.

Promise walked away smiling thinking how the Queen term threw her off. It threw most females off. He didn't understand why women didn't know their rightful place in a man's life. It didn't matter either way. That was their hang up, as long as when the time came Divine knew her place in his.

As he walked away he saw his OG Pops and decided to stop and holla at him for a sec.

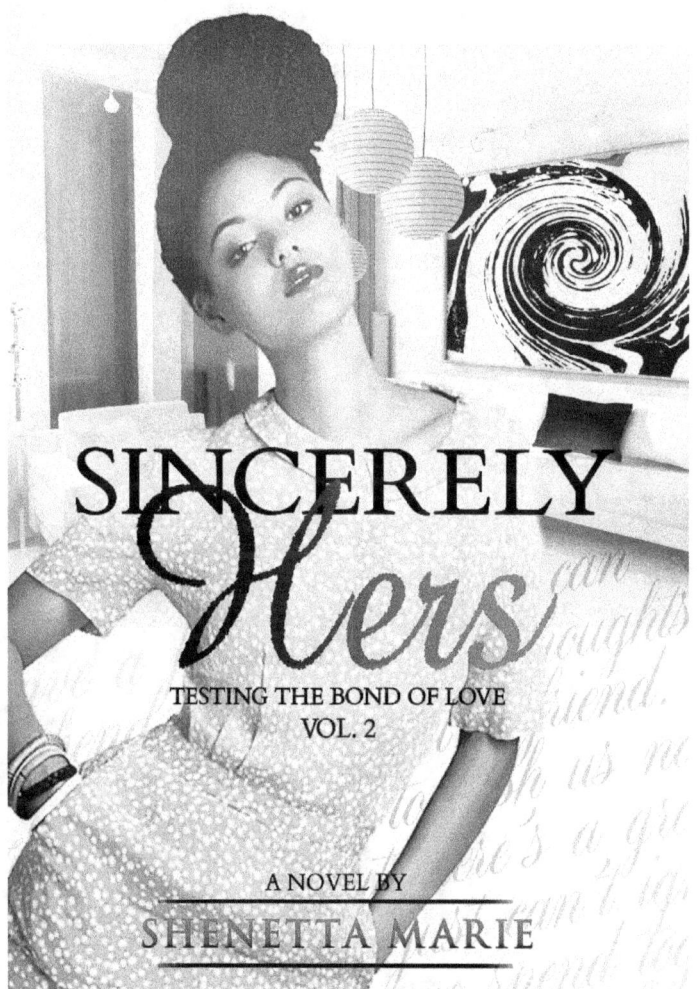

A DIVINE PRODUCTION PRESENTS

SINCERELY
Hers

TESTING THE BOND OF LOVE
VOL. 2

A NOVEL BY

SHENETTA MARIE

Available Now

A DIVINE PRODUCTION PRESENTS

Her

THE CONCLUSION

WILL LOVE SURVIVE ON THE STREETS OF THE LAND

VOL. 3

A NOVEL BY

SHENETTA MARIE

Available Now

About the author

Shenetta Marie born and raised in Cleveland, Ohio, is a mother of two wonderful sons. She loves to spend time with her family and close friends and is now embracing her new love, writing.

Feel free to visit the rising Author/Publisher @
shenettamarie@yahoo.com
Follow her on twitter @shenettamarie
facebook Author Shenetta Marie
IG @shenettamarie